Destroying Dominic

Genoa Mafia Series Book III

By Ginger Ring

Destroying Dominic

Limitless Publishing, LLC
Kailua, HI 96734
www.limitlesspublishing.com

Formatting: Limitless Publishing

ISBN-13: 978-1-64034-449-5
ISBN-10: 1-64034-449-7

Prologue

Anastasia

A flash of lightning lit up the sky. It'd been storming all evening but the rain had so far held off. It was unusual weather for southern California, but then everything had seemed off lately.

"I don't know about this. What if we get caught?" Marina stomped her high heeled foot.

"We won't get caught." Stassi pulled her two friends along. "Come on. This will be so much fun." They ignored the claps of thunder as they stood on the corner.

Marina wouldn't move. "Stassi, you know you aren't allowed to be out by yourself. Your father will be furious if he finds out. Plus, we should be studying for finals."

"That's exactly why we need to do this. Soon, you'll both be working full-time jobs and I'll be getting married. Don't you want to have some fun

1

before you have to settle down?"

Lord knew she did. Sure, Maksim, her intended, was nice and her father treated him like a son whenever he was around, but the guy was all business. The same family business that she'd grown up in. The mafia business. What it all entailed she'd never be privy to or even wanted to know. It just meant that her father was a big deal around town and she was never without a bodyguard.

She'd witnessed men come into the house and never leave, or they exited the place with bloody faces and cracked ribs. She'd sneaked around, seen things she shouldn't have. Her father always wanted a son, but that wasn't to be. The man pretty much ignored her ever since her mother died so many years ago. Her value only lie in who she would marry and the alliance that union would make. Maksim was from a high-ranking family, the best, and it was only a matter of time before they were hitched.

It also meant that her life wasn't her own. At eighteen, she'd still never been out by herself, gone to a club, or even had a date except for the ones arranged with Maksim and under the supervision of their fathers. They were rivals, so, of course, their children must marry to officially bind their families, even if she didn't want any part of it. It was her duty.

Stassi shivered. Recently, when others weren't watching, she'd noticed Maksim staring at her like she was prey. It was in her nature to not judge others, but he seemed to have a dark vibe surrounding him. Being around him was not one of her favorite things to do. They had zero in common. One time, he was at their house for dinner and she joked about his fancy shoes. She was just trying to break the ice and say something funny, but Maksim was so insulted he snapped at her. The air was hot and humid yet a chill ran up her spine.

"I'm sorry, Stassi." Sarah's lip stuck out and she draped an arm over Stassi's shoulder.

"About what? Don't tell me you're chickening out also." Dang it, she didn't want to go by herself, but there was no way she was going to sit at home with her dad finally out of town. It was rare that she could sneak off unnoticed.

"No, I'll go. I'm just sorry that you are marrying Maksim. You're far too young."

He wasn't the most handsome, that was for sure, but looks didn't make a marriage. She would be well taken care of. His family had more money than hers, and that was saying something. She'd be upgrading her gilded cage for a golden one.

"You know what the deal is." Stassi shrugged. Sarah and Marina were friends from school who knew about her family and that she was contracted to marry. They could marry for love. Her, not so much. "Please, let's go. If we don't get there in time, the limo will be full and they'll leave without us."

They'd taken an Uber to the address that was on the card.

"So how did you find out about this?" Marina finally got in line behind a half dozen girls.

They were all laughing and sporting short, low-cut dresses. The outfits of these girls made theirs look like they were going to church. What did hookers wear these days? It couldn't be less than what they had on. Stassi rolled her eyes.

"I overheard the guys talking about this place. That it was a hidden nightclub. Only the best are allowed in. You have to have one of these cards to get in. I snatched one when they weren't looking." She waved it in front of their faces. "It's so secret you have to hand over your phone until the end of the night. They don't want photos getting out. I wonder if there'll be any celebrities there."

The young women squealed when a black stretch limo pulled up. A handsome young man in a suit got out of the passenger side and walked up to them. A few girls swooned and giggled.

"Ladies, my name is Luis. You're all looking very lovely this evening. I hope you all have your cards with you." He held out a box and winked at the first one in line. "Please drop those and your phones in here."

Marina touched Anastasia's arm. "I still don't like this."

Stassi reached for a strand of hair to twirl around her finger. "I promise. Everything will be fine. If we don't have any fun, we'll go home and watch a movie. Okay?"

Her friend nodded and smiled but it was forced.

It seemed like a good idea at the time, but now doubts edged into her mind.

"Hello. Please drop your cards and phones in here," Luis repeated as he walked down the line. The man wasn't as good looking up close and his cologne burned her nose. Stassi held out the business card and dropped it and her phone in the box. He nodded toward the limo. "Thanks, beautiful. You'll never forget this night. As soon as you're all in, we'll be on our way."

"Let's go. It's going to be a blast. I just know it," she reassured her friends, and Stassi herded them toward the vehicle like a mother hen.

The other girls in the limo didn't seem the least bit nervous and were busy passing a bottle of tequila and some red plastic cups around. Stassi declined but Marina and Sarah each took a sip. They weren't twenty-one, but no one seemed to care. They traveled for about fifteen minutes through dark alleys and empty parking lots. It was as if they were trying to make sure no one knew where they were going.

Stassi peeked out the darkened windows a few times. No one else paid any attention to the neighborhoods they were in. The vehicle slowed and she studied the surroundings—they seemed to be in a warehouse district. Maybe Marina was right, but all Stassi wanted was to have a little fun, escape her life for a few hours. Stassi wrung her hands as lightning illuminated their dismal surroundings.

The car finally stopped outside a two-story concrete building. This time, Luis and the driver both waited outside for them. The building pulsated with loud music coming from inside. A couple girls jumped up and down. That seemed to calm her a bit. Maybe the place was legit.

Luis opened the door to the building and the latest dance tune boomed as disco lights flashed in the distance. The girls crowded in, with Stassi, Marina, and Sarah trailing behind. It was dimly lit but there was a long hallway ahead. Everyone rushed for the music and bright party lights that came from the end of the corridor.

Stepping into the main room, they all stopped and gawked. It was just an empty room. Something wasn't right. Where was the DJ, the dancers? This was supposed to be a club. Were they the first ones there? The girls wandered around, confused.

The music stopped and the lights were flipped on. Blindingly bright lights. A few questioned what was going on. Marina and Sarah clung on each side of Stassi.

"I knew this was wrong," Marina cried. "Oh god."

"What's this about?" Stassi spoke up. "Where's the party?"

Luis smirked and strolled up to her. His hand tightly gripped her face and Stassi grimaced. "You stupid little girls are the party."

Gasps filled the air.

Before they knew it, men came out of the shadows. The girls scattered like ants but it was no use. The men tied the girls' wrists behind their backs and held them all standing in place in a circle. Some started to sob or call for help. Stassi shook her head, eager to wake from this bad dream. Only there was no rousing from it; she was living a true nightmare.

Her friends were pulled from her side and each held by a brut. Some wore bandannas covering their faces like they were about to rob a bank. Unlike

Luis, these captives were dressed in leather cuts and jeans. Bikers. Her mind worked overtime trying to remember every detail to figure out why this was happening. Every detail was tagged and logged in her brain, including their shoes. The man who held her captive had a big handlebar mustache.

"Silence, everyone," Luis shouted until they quieted, but some of the girls still sobbed. The storm outside rivaled the chaos inside. The thunder was now a constant rumble. A lone figure stepped into the middle of the room. His face was also covered but the change of mannerisms from the others clearly showed he was the one in charge.

"Ladies, I'm sorry your evening isn't going to go as you planned." The man quickly walked to each of the girls, looking them up and down. A few he struggled with and roughly lifted their chins to see them better. Stassi kept her head down as he passed by her. "From this day forward, your lives will, unfortunately," he paused, "never be the same." He went back to the center of the room and started pointing. Something about the man was familiar, but she couldn't put her finger on it.

"Take this one, this one, and those three to Vlad, and the rest to Igor." The room went crazy as bags were thrown over the girls' heads and they were dragged kicking and screaming from the room. Stassi glanced at her two friends. The pain and fear on Marina's face would haunt her forever. She couldn't move as they were both dragged away. Stassi's heart pounded in her chest. This couldn't be happening. When her vision went black from the bag, it jerked her into action. Stassi struggled as

7

best she could in a dress and high heels.

Heavy rain pelted the roof as tears streamed down her face.

"Wait," the boss shouted, and the man holding her stilled. Stassi felt warm fingers touch the back of her neck as someone brushed her hair away and tore the sack off her head. A deep laugh rumbled behind her and a hand reached around her neck. The lights flickered as lightning struck outside. The sound of thunder was deafening but she heard every word he said.

"This one stays with me."

Her gaze fell to the floor. She finally recognized the voice and the shoes. They both belonged to Maksim.

Chapter One

Stephanie

It was a good wedding as far as weddings go. The couple was an unlikely pair. Valentina Caponelli, the daughter of one of the biggest mafia dons in Chicago, had married Ryan Donavan, one of Genoa's police officers. Opposites really did attract.

Stephanie Barclay surveyed the festivities from across the dimly lit ballroom. The wedding had taken place at a lakeside estate belonging to Roman Caponelli, the brother of the bride. The reception and dance had progressed to Firenza, the restaurant and event center that the bride ran. Valentina was also a lawyer—to say the woman was an overachiever would be an understatement.

By anyone's standards, this had been a very high-end celebration. The gown had been designed and made by the bride's sister-in-law, Madison Caponelli. Maddy could have been a highly paid designer of couture gowns but she'd given it up to marry into the mob. Yes, love was blind, deaf, and totally messed one up.

If Stephanie thought about it too much, her head might explode. She'd done her best to get away from that kind of people and now she was right back in the middle of them. The Caponellis would be shocked to know how she'd been raised. To everyone here, she was just a drifter, a summer tourist who'd stayed. How very wrong they all were.

Before meeting Roman, Madison had run the Bells and Bows Bridal store for years. When Stephanie passed the shop with a help wanted sign in the window, the rest was history. Since Madison's marriage, all the responsibility had fallen on Steph's shoulders. It was her job today to keep everything running smoothly, and, so far, it had gone like clockwork.

She reached for a strand of hair to twirl around her finger but her hair was up. Stephanie took a deep breath. Every moment here was torture. Funny how it never bothered her to help plan a wedding at the shop, but this was different. It brought back raw memories.

All the traditions that were so important to the festivities now rubbed her like sandpaper. Maybe it was just jealousy. Envy for something that would never happen, could never happen. Her trust was gone. Her identity was that of someone else. Her life was one day after another of looking over her shoulder in the hopes that it wasn't her last. A couple couldn't keep secrets from each other, and she had more than most. No sense dating when you couldn't even tell someone your real name.

It was almost midnight. Thankfully, there was only one more hour and then she could help with clean up. The staff was wonderful, but someone still needed to oversee things. At least the gifts could stay here. The Caponellis owned Firenza, and no one would dare steal them. She snagged a glass of champagne off a tray as a server passed by and downed it in one sip. It was time to go to work and cross another tradition off the list. Stephanie tucked a box under her arm and hurried to the bride.

Valentina was talking to an older woman, and Steph tapped her on the shoulder. "I hate to interrupt, but it's time to toss the bouquet."

"Oh, yes." Val turned and hugged the woman. "Thank you for coming, Aunt Camille. I'm so happy you could share this special day with us."

"It's my pleasure, dear." Camille kissed the bride's cheek and left the two girls alone.

"Let me see it." Valentina clasped her hands together in front of her chest.

Stephanie opened the box that held the throw bouquet. Whereas Valentina's elegant bouquet was made up of fire and ice roses, this one was simpler. "It's lovely." A whiff of lavender caught her nose as Steph pulled it from the tissue of the box. It was a collection of wildflowers in yellows, pinks, purples, and oranges.

"I thought you'd like it. I made it with you in mind, that's why you have to catch it," Valentina declared.

Stephanie handed the bouquet to the bride. "Oh, no. Thanks, but I'm not interested."

"You have to." Valentina frowned for the first time that day.

"I just don't believe in that stuff." Weddings and riding off into the sunset were for other people.

"Humor me, okay?"

Stephanie shook her head.

Several giggling young women gathered near the stage. Madison waved her over to the group but Steph's feet remained locked in place. Finally, the maid of honor, with a nod from the bride, rushed over and led Stephanie by the arm to the group of single women.

"Come on. I know you'll be next. I can feel it," Madison insisted. Her friends were determined to get her hitched. It was the last thing she wanted or needed right now. Not only was it stupid, it was dangerous for any man to get involved with her. If anyone took up with her, he would have to be fearless and good with a gun.

"That's called a buzz. You've probably just had too much to drink." Stephanie brushed it off but faked some enthusiasm anyway. She'd been playacting for so long, it was hard to know who she really was anymore. If one thing was true, it was that she really did care for Madison and Valentina. The rest she kept at arm's length.

"The only thing I'm drunk on is happiness, and I want that for you too." Madison and Roman had been married almost a year and yet they still acted like newlyweds. They were just too much to be around at times.

She rolled her eyes and quelled the need to do the finger in her mouth gag bit.

Maddy kissed her on the cheek and whispered in her ear, "You will be next. So catch the damn flowers. It's an order."

Before Stephanie knew it, Maddy was gone and she was nudged from behind as the crowd edged closer to the bride. There was no way she would get in anyone's way. She stepped to the side, turned toward the bar, and her heart to skip a beat.

There sat the only man who could turn her head. Why he did, she had no clue. Dominic Scarlatti was dangerous, did horrible things for a living, and was one of the most beautiful men she'd ever laid eyes on.

Usually, he dressed like an outdoorsman, in flannel shirts and jeans, but tonight he was in a pair of dress pants, a jacket, and a button-down shirt. His long hair was up in a bun. She'd tried to block him from her view most of the night, but when he was in sight, there was usually a girl or two beside him. The guy was a loner, but you couldn't blame the ladies for trying. The area was now empty except for Dom and his boss, Roman. Madison joined the pair as they watched the festivities.

Whack. Out of nowhere, something bounced off her chest and she instinctively grabbed for it. The group of girls groaned while Madison and Valentina jumped for joy. The bride ran over to lift Steph's arm in the air like she'd just won a prize fight.

"What the…?" She'd caught the dreaded bouquet.

"I knew it." Valentina gleamed and pressed one hand over her heart.

"This was fixed," Stephanie argued and held the

13

flowers to her nose. They were really pretty and would brighten up her dingy apartment. The place hadn't been updated since the fifties. The sleazy place she rented only allowed cash payments—no paper trail.

"Hey. My back was turned," Valentina said. "I couldn't see where I was throwing it, but you were meant to have it. If anyone deserves happiness, it's you."

"Thank you." She hugged the bride. Maddy and Val really did mean well, and she was lucky to have them both.

"Now to find you a groom." Valentina wiggled her eyebrows before returning to her spot by the stage where Ryan now waited.

Madison returned and hooked her arm with Steph's. They took a seat at a nearby table. It was now the guys' turn. Everyone watched as the bride took a seat by the platform. The band played a frisky tune while her new husband slipped the garter from her leg. The bachelors started to gather.

Ryan stood with his back to the crowd. He twirled the bit of lace around on his finger before letting it fly. A few guys jumped to snatch it, but one large hand easily grasped it from the air. The room went quiet when everyone noticed the tall man with the garter in his hand. It was the cleaner for the mob, Dominic Scarlatti. A devilish grin crossed his lips. The man stuffed the garter in his pocket and walked back to the bar.

"Well, that was interesting." Madison motioned for one of the waiters to bring them a drink. "He really is a good guy, Steph. Despite, well, you know."

"On what planet is a guy who makes people disappear considered good?" Stephanie took the drink that was offered. It'd been a long day; she'd sleep well tonight. At least tomorrow was Sunday, so she didn't have to work.

Madison shrugged. "Someone has to do it."

"Wow, you've sure changed your tune." Stephanie crossed her legs and flexed her toes. How could Valentina wear high heels every day? Her feet were killing her.

"Well, I'm the first to admit that marrying into the mob has changed my view on a lot of things." Not many people knew Roman had come to the rescue when Madison had been kidnapped by the abusive fiancé of one of their brides.

Madison convinced the woman to call things off and the man did not take it well. With Roman's help, the man was no longer a threat or abusing women. Still, it didn't make what Roman and his men did any better. "All I can say is that love changes things." Her husband came up behind her and placed a hand on her shoulder, which she soon covered with her own. "I've never been happier."

If Roman hadn't been staring down at her with those all-knowing eyes, she'd have made a smart-aleck remark. Steph didn't mess with the man. It was like he knew she had secrets. Every time he was around, it was as if he was watching her, studying her for a misstep or the glimpse of a clue to who she really was. He saw right through her. Roman didn't get where he was without being smart and one step ahead of the rest. The guy was on to her.

"I'd like to dance with my wife." His low, deep voice could still be heard above the loud music.

"My pleasure." Madison rose and wrapped her arms around her husband's neck.

Stephanie took another sip of her drink and watched the dancers for the next half hour. The clock now read twelve thirty; soon, it would all be over with. She hid a yawn with her hand. The bouquet sat on the table in front of her. Someone else should have caught it. Someone who actually wanted it. Stephanie jerked in her seat. *Oh crap.* It was tradition that the man who caught the garter dance with the woman who caught the flowers. Did Dom know about that?

"Excuse me," a husky voice said in her ear. Stephanie jumped and turned in her chair. "Would you care to dance?"

The air left her chest, whether from relief or disappointment, it was hard to tell. It was Jasper. They'd never officially met but she knew who he was. The young soldier in the Caponelli family had occasionally driven Madison around since Arlo had been working in Chicago for Roman's father from time to time. As the saying went, if you couldn't beat them, dance with them. "Uh, sure," she mumbled, and let him lead her to the dance floor.

Jasper was a good dancer and not hard on the eyes. Was it a requirement that all bad boys be handsome, or did the fact that they did bad things just appeal to some sick, twisted part of her? The guy was a player, that was easy to see. Jasper was looking for someone to take home for the night, but that wouldn't be her. They waltzed around the floor with a smile and nod to the other couples.

There was no use denying it though, her gaze was on the search for someone else. The mystery man who never failed to intrigue her. What had possessed Dominic to play along with the crowd and catch the bride's garter? He was the last person in the world she'd expect to see here, let alone participate.

It was no use trying to get him out of her mind. The man had taken up residency a few months ago. Dominic had been there when no one else was. He had been there when she needed someone to protect her, someone to comfort her, and someone to kill and bury a body for her.

Chapter Two

Dominic

Earlier That Day

Many people thought they had a shitty job, but until they've had to clean up a couple dead bodies that have been sitting in a hot trailer for a few days, they should consider themselves lucky.

"God, it stinks in here." Jasper gagged and Dominic tossed him a mask.

"It's a meth lab with two corpses, what'd you think it'd smell like? I've seen and smelled worse." This was why he liked to work alone. No complaining, no whining, and no small talk. Just him. "Why are you here anyway?"

Jasper was a new guy. He was one of those eager beavers who wanted to move up the ranks fast and was willing to do most anything to accomplish that goal. From what'd he heard when Jasper was in Chicago, he'd do a hit, party at the clubs all night, and still be fresh-faced in the morning. He also had a reputation with the ladies. Love them and leave them. There were probably broken hearts all over the Windy City when he left town. The prick should have stayed there.

"Roman wanted me to help so you could get done early and go to his sister's wedding." The guy kicked over a chair and Dom gritted his teeth.

"Don't touch anything," Dominic barked. Just what he needed, some idiot trying to rush his ass so he could get to a stupid wedding on time. A wedding was the last place he wanted to be, but he owed everything to the Caponellis. Roman and Valentina may not have been blood, but they were the only family he had. Dominic would kill and die for them. If Roman wanted him to be at the wedding, he'd do his best to be there with or without Jasper's help. Unfortunately, this smell didn't come off easily and it was only getting worse the longer they stayed.

He turned as Jasper tipped over a shelving unit. What was wrong with this jerk? They were far out in the country, but what if someone heard all the noise?

"Hey, dickhead. I told you not to touch anything."

"What's the difference? We're going to torch it anyway." The man acted like he was searching for a place to sit or lean but didn't want to get his fancy suit dirty. The last thing Dom needed was a distraction. Distractions made one sloppy, and sloppiness led to missing things. Things that law enforcement or fire investigators might find later.

"Yes, and we want it to look like these tweakers

did it themselves. Not that the place was trashed before it burned. Put everything back where you found it." Meth labs were highly flammable, so it wasn't uncommon for them to catch fire.

With a loud exhale, the guy did as he was told. "Are we going to leave these guys here?" He nodded to the two dead bodies on the floor. Flies buzzed and maggots crawled around the grizzly scene.

"Yeah, we just have to make sure we have all the bullets and casings that might be lying around." They'd already found three casings by the door. One guy had been shot in the head so that one was easy to locate. He rolled the other guy over on his side. There was an entry wound but the bullet hadn't gone all the way through. If he'd been shot where he fell, that meant the other bullet might be behind him. "Check for any holes over there." Dom pointed a gloved finger toward the wall behind Jasper.

"What happened here anyway?" Jasper traced a finger along the cheap paneling.

"Roman doesn't allow drugs to be sold in Genoa. He made a deal with a biker gang that does. As long as they don't sell within the town limits, he'll help keep the competition out."

"I saw their bikes out front. Who killed these guys and why are we cleaning them up?"

"These guys don't belong to that club. They moved into the territory, so we had to take them out. Not sure who the hell they are but our tech guys already have their photos and everything off their phones. We'll know soon enough."

"Hey, I found it." Jasper took out a knife and dug a bullet from its hole in the wall. "That makes two, where's the other one?"

"It's still in him." Dom rolled the man back to the floor.

"How're we going to get it out?"

"How do you think?" Dominic grabbed a pair of long nose pliers. Now he had to dig around until he found the metal. All in a day's work.

Jasper strolled over to a window, peeled back the newspaper that covered it, and looked outside.

The smell was even worse when he opened the guy up, but Dom barely noticed. It took a bit but he finally located the piece of metal they were searching for.

"Are we done yet?" Jasper griped.

Damn. Would the guy ever shut up? "What is your problem? You got a hot date or something?"

"I've got to get cleaned up and then I'm going to the reception."

Yeah, the pretty boy would be on the prowl. "We have one more thing to do before we set the place on fire." Dominic got to his feet. With some bleach, he cleaned and then put away all the tools he'd brought along.

"Oh yeah? What's that?" Jasper put the paper back in place and turned around.

"If the guy's skull stays intact, an investigator will be able to see the bullet hole. We need something to fall on his head and smash it."

"That's easy." Jasper strolled over and kicked the wooden leg of a nearby table. A microwave slipped off and landed on the drug dealer's head, making a sickening crunch. It was one of those huge old ones that weighed a ton. The thing got the job done. Maybe Jasper wasn't such an idiot after all. "Now the fun part." He clapped his hands together and wiggled his eyebrows. "Where's the gasoline?"

"No, that can be seen in the way it burns. Take all the paper off the windows and stuff it in the areas I tell you. Then we light a match. A lot of matches. The chemicals will do the rest."

It didn't take long before the place was ablaze. They waited in the van down the road to make sure it took hold and wasn't going to stop. Dominic untied his long hair and put the vehicle in drive. Damn, the smell was in his hair. He'd need a long shower, but it took forever for his thick hair to dry.

He yawned and slipped a pair of sunglasses on. It was sunny and a perfect day for a wedding. Dominic would pass on the ceremony but he'd make an appearance later. There was no hurry and he needed a bit of time to himself. Crowds emotionally and physically drained him. Peace and solitude were more to his liking.

"Shit, I'm going to have to burn these." Jasper took a whiff of his sleeve. "I love this suit."

Dom grunted. Who wore good clothes to a crime scene? Dominic was the cleaner for the Caponelli family. That meant he cleaned up whatever messes were left behind. Whatever that may be. Since moving to Genoa, that part of his job was few and far between. Now he was often a bodyguard or a driver for family members. The knot in his gut signaled that after today, that part of his job was going to pick up again.

"So, are you going?" His passenger kept yakking.

"Going to what?" Dominic stopped at the intersection. He had to be careful to always obey traffic laws in this business. He didn't want to be stopped for a violation with a body in the back. He was also obsessive about checking his brake and headlights before going on a job. Keeping license registration up to date was a must as well.

Jasper let out a big sigh. "The wedding. Jeez."

"No, but I'll show up for the dance." Dominic would be there about ten minutes before it ended. That would be enough. With any luck, most of the partygoers would be gone by then. "What are you so excited about?"

"Chicks, man. I'm hoping to get lucky. All I've done is work since I got here. It's time to hook up with the ladies." Jasper crossed his ankle over his knee. "Got my eye on one too. Pretty blonde."

"Oh yeah?" Dom made a mental note to tell Roman from now on he only worked alone. He had no interest in hearing about Jasper's conquests.

"Yeah. You must know her too. Stephanie Barclay, that blonde who works at the bridal shop. Boy, I'd love to have her…"

Dominic hit the brake harder than intended at the turnoff and Jasper slid into the dash. His skull bumped the window. "What the hell?" He rubbed his head.

"Sorry, but you should be wearing a seatbelt. I don't want to be stopped by some cop." Sorry— that's what Jasper would be if he ever dared touched a single hair on Stephanie's head.

The guy snapped the belt in place. "She's a beauty, and with her being best friends with Roman's wife, it might score me some points with the boss. From what I've heard, they've been trying to fix her up for some time." Jasper cracked his knuckles. "And I'm just the guy to bring home the goods."

Dominic pulled off the road and grabbed his passenger by the collar. "If you ever lay one finger on her, I will take your arm. Got it?" He stared him right in the eye.

"What the hell? Easy." Jasper held his hands up. "Sorry, didn't know she was yours."

Dom shoved him back in the seat. "She's not mine. I just don't want to see her hurt."

"I have no intentions of hurting any woman. Just wanted some company." Jasper sulked and crossed his arms over his chest. "Cockblocker."

"I don't give a shit who you spend time with, but she's off limits." If only that were true, but he had no real say. From the first time he laid eyes on her, there was something about Stephanie that grabbed at his heart. She was vulnerable, yet he knew everyone underestimated her strength. The woman was stunning yet underplayed her looks. It was as if she wanted to go through life being unnoticed and unseen. He knew she had secrets, but what they were was anyone's guess.

They did share one skeleton in the closet, but he didn't want to think about that right now. He was more concerned with someone putting the moves on her. Dammit, now he was going to have to show up earlier to keep his eyes on her. "They don't want her mixed up with any of the help."

"Really?" Jasper smirked. "Why's she off limits if just the other day Madison was telling me I should ask her out?"

Dominic counted the miles and minutes until he could get rid of Jasper and his questions. It twisted his gut that Maddy would encourage someone else to take her out. Had she done that with him? He couldn't remember. Valentina mentioned the two of them getting together a few times, but he'd always brushed it off. Maybe they'd just given up on him. It was his fault if they did. Dom was a loner and a freak on the border of polite society, to put it mildly. She was too good for him, that was for sure. Any woman would consider themselves too good for the likes of him and what he did and what he'd done in the past.

Sure, Dom knew he was good looking. There were always chicks looking for a walk on the dangerous side, and he'd taken good advantage of that in Chicago. In the small town of Genoa, that was a different matter. You didn't shit where you ate. There were business and social connections, and he preferred to stay on the fringes of both. Most importantly, having a woman made a person weak. Enemies would strike what you loved first and come at you second. He knew that firsthand and would be haunted by that until his dying day.

"Well?" Jasper piped up again. "I'm waiting."

There it was again, the annoying noise of his passenger asking stupid questions he didn't know the answer to.

"Look, I don't know. Just leave her alone. She's

a nice girl." With an unknown past, Dom left out.

"I like nice girls," Jasper said.

"Fuck." Dom waved him the middle finger. "If you say one more word, you can walk the rest of the way."

"Whatever." Jasper sunk low in his seat like a spoiled teenager but at least he shut up.

The rest of the trip was thankfully done in silence, and he dropped Jasper off at the guy's apartment downtown. It irritated him that it was only a few blocks from where Stephanie lived. Not that he was stalking her or anything, but he drove by her place anyway. It was a two-story building with eight apartments, four on the bottom floor and four on the top. She'd be at the wedding at this hour but he needed to see it just the same. A woman like her shouldn't be living alone in a place like that. Though Dominic knew it was a good bet that the other residents who lived there were just as secretive as she was.

Dominic slowed when he spied a man leave the back wearing a motorcycle club cut. He parked the van on the side of the street and retrieved his binoculars from the glove compartment. It wasn't a club from around Genoa. As if an afterthought, the man stopped and glanced around before slipping out of the cut and stuffing it in one of his saddlebags. Was he in the same group as the meth heads they'd just left?

That didn't sit well with Dom, and he placed the binoculars on the seat. The man started his bike and eased it out onto the street. As the motorcycle cruised by, Dominic entered the man's California license plates on his phone. A cloud seemed to drift over the otherwise beautiful day. The biker he'd killed a couple months ago to protect Stephanie was also from the sunshine state.

Chapter Three

He wasn't much of a social drinker, but Dominic made an exception when surrounded by this many people. So much for slipping in at the end of the night, he'd barely taken time to shower and change before cruising to Firenza. He'd missed the dinner but didn't turn down the cake. Taking a sip of whiskey, he leaned an elbow on the bar and turned toward the dance floor.

It was usually quiet when he visited the place. Roman had an office there when he didn't want to bring associates to his house. Dominic had been here many times and knew the place as well as any of the workers. Tonight, it was noisy and crowded, two of his least favorite things.

Firenza had been an old gangster haunt at one time, and technically still was. The place was far enough away from the lake that there were tunnels under it where they used to store bootleg whiskey during Prohibition. Roman's employees still used it to hide things they didn't want found and it was rumored a ghost of someone buried there years ago roamed the passageways.

Tonight, the place was decorated in blue and red. White Christmas lights and netting hung from the ceiling and lit up the tables. There were red rose centerpieces everywhere. He'd never bought any flowers but guessed that alone had cost a fortune.

"Been fishing much?" the bartender asked as he pulled on the tap for a beer. His name was Trevor and he'd seen the guy out on the lake a couple times.

"Nah, been busy, maybe next week." He liked fishing. It was quiet. Not many people around. It wasn't like being at the freaking wedding.

"I like to fish," a young woman in a low-cut fire-red dress slurred.

"Good for you." Dom turned away. The last thing he needed was some drunken long-lost cousin of the bride or groom looking for a good time. Where was that ass Jasper when he needed him?

The music stopped and everyone turned their attention to the stage. Valentina stood waiting for all the single women to line up. He chuckled to himself as Maddy dragged a reluctant Stephanie to the group. She craved attention as much as he did.

Valentina was a beautiful bride and Madison was equally attractive, but in his eyes, Steph was the clear winner in the looks department. The woman was tall and shapely. Not as tall as he, of course, but not a petite little thing. She was curvy in all the right places. Despite the shyness she portrayed, the woman was strong and fierce. He'd seen it firsthand. She would never go down without a fight, and that was the kind of woman he wanted and needed.

What the hell? Dom glanced at the drink in his hand. It was whiskey, not absinthe. Since when did he need anyone? He preferred to be alone, thrived on it, in fact. Groans of disappointment brought his eyes back to the dance floor. It was Stephanie who'd caught the bouquet, indicating she would be the next to marry. Over his dead body, she would. Again, he stared at his drink. Who she dated was no concern of his, but thinking of her with someone else bothered him. It knocked him in the gut. He'd been void of feelings for longer than he could remember, yet just the sight of her calmed him, warmed him from the inside out. It was nice but concerning at the same time. Feelings were for normal people. He wasn't one of them.

Her blonde hair shimmered in the lights as she tipped her head to smell the colorful flowers. They were more her style than the roses. As if he was a flower expert now, but they suited her and a smile lit up her face. The heat in his heart turned up a notch.

Stephanie was different than everyone there. Whereas the other chicks wore skin-tight dresses that would have to be peeled off with a can opener, hers was off the shoulder and flowy. Her long blonde hair was up with little flowers poked in here and there. Others wore flashy jewels around their necks and ears. He noticed she preferred bracelets. Other times he'd seen her sport ones of leather and beads, tonight, they were simple gold.

The woman with the red dress and stripper shoes returned to the bar. A big frown was on her lips.

"Better luck next time," he tossed out.

"Think you can do any better," she challenged and narrowed her eyes, "go ahead."

It was on the tip of his tongue to decline when he noticed Jasper joining the group of bachelors hoping to catch the bride's garter. Why did people care about these stupid traditions anyway? Then again, it would give that loser a reason to go talk to her if he caught it. *Son of a bitch.* This drink was spiked with something.

Not bothering to respond, he left his tainted love potion on the bar and slid, unnoticed, over to the group of guys. Ryan let it soar and the little bit of lace flew over the heads of most of those gathered. Dom reached up and easily caught it on the fly. Amongst all the groans, he stuffed it in his pocket and wandered back to the bar. The music started again and he settled into his seat.

Red dress lady was thankfully gone from sight. The bartender waited with a fresh glass. Thank god. "Congratulations, you're the next to get hitched."

"Yeah, tell me another story." He took the shot and slammed the glass upside down on the wood. "I just did it to prove a point."

"And you can dance with the girl who caught the flowers." Trevor wiggled his eyebrows.

"I don't dance, but I might." Dom exhaled. It was a losing battle as far as she was concerned. As much as he tried to stay away, he craved her like a bad habit.

"Well, you'd better hurry. Looks like someone already beat you to it." The guy pointed with the towel he had in hand.

31

There on the dance floor was Jasper with Stephanie in his arms. That son of a bitch! He should have thrown him out of the van and run him over when he had a chance.

"So what are you going to do about it?" Trevor rested his elbows on the bar.

"Something I shouldn't," he said under his breath.

Dominic weaved in and out of the couples dancing. It was his bad luck that the pair he searched for was now on the far side of the room. At one point he lost sight of them and panic set in. He'd made it a point to avoid her for the last couple months, but seeing her tonight just caused the attraction to return. In the middle of the floor, he stopped. Where were they? A few dump sites for Jasper's corpse flashed before his eyes.

Finally, he caught a glimpse of her pretty hair and quickly headed their way. Jasper was damn lucky he hadn't tried anything. It was bad enough he was touching her, if things went any farther, he'd have to kill the guy. No questions asked.

Dominic hesitated. He'd always been a person who shunned contact with people, yet she was different. Stephanie was the only woman to ever step a foot into his house except for Madison, and that was just to pick her up. His home was his sanctuary, his asylum from a boisterous world. It was the one place he could get away from people. She'd only spent one stormy night there but her presence still lingered

"Hell." Dom stomped toward the couple and tapped Jasper on the shoulder. "My turn," he shouted over the music, and he could see Stephanie's green eyes widen.

"Only if it's okay with the lady." Jasper nodded toward the woman in his arms.

Her lower lip quivered and she finally said yes.

"Well then, thanks for the dance." Jasper smiled and then whispered in Dom's ear, "Took you long enough." He then disappeared into the crowd.

The music stopped and then restarted with a slower tune. Fuck. He hated dancing. What was the point? Had he ever danced with a woman? Dom couldn't recall. Finally, Stephanie stepped closer and took one hand in hers and rested the other on his arm. Her touch reassured him, called to him.

The corners of her mouth turned up. "I never pictured you for a dancer."

"I'm not." He stood firm. "Can we sit down?"

"No." The woman could be stubborn, it seemed. She was in his arms, so why not enjoy it. He wasn't ready to let her go anyway. He wrapped one around her waist and pulled her closer. They didn't take any steps but that was fine with him. "You look beautiful tonight." The woman always did, even when she wasn't trying, which was most days.

"So do you. I mean, you look handsome." Stephanie blushed and then laid her head on his shoulder. Was she embarrassed about what she said and wanted to hide? All that mattered was that she was pressed against his chest. The woman was an angel in the arms of the devil. Her scent was light and fresh. Not some heavy perfume like that chick at the bar. She smelled like the wildflowers that grew around his home. He breathed deeply in the hopes it would lock in his memory for some long, sleepless night.

They didn't drift much from the spot, just moved back and forth where they were. It was as if they were in their own little world and didn't want to be disturbed.

All too soon the music ended and the lights flickered on. They stepped back, dropped their hands, and let their eyes adjust to the brightness. Stephanie wet her lips and glanced everywhere but toward him. "Uh, thanks for the dance."

"I don't dance." He tried to deny it again.

"Yeah, well, whatever. I have to get back to work," Stephanie mumbled and looked at the floor.

"Work? It's over with now." He watched Ryan and Valentina shaking hands and hugging their guests goodbye.

"Yes, but I have to stay and make sure everything is cleaned up before I can leave."

"Don't they have people for that?" They'd really not talked at all since what happened a couple months ago, but it needed to be done. Whether he wanted to or not.

"I am one of those people. Excuse me, I have to speak with Val before they leave."

"I'll go with you." Dominic motioned for her to lead the way. He'd never been one to stare at a woman, but he couldn't get enough of the gorgeous blonde who'd just left his arms. She had a long, elegant neck and the off the shoulder dress highlighted her tan skin. How he yearned to reach out and see if her skin was as soft and smooth as it appeared. There was a tattoo on the back of her neck but it was hard to make out what it was. Did she have any others? Jeez, he was following her like a love-sick puppy, and that needed to end. As soon as he touched base with her about the biker, he was gone. Out of there and back to his quiet place.

"Dom." Roman came out of nowhere and stopped him in his tracks. "Everything go all right today?"

"Yeah." He focused his eyes on Stephanie's ass as she kept walking.

"Did Jasp help?" The man had a drink in one hand and his other arm wrapped around his wife.

"Yes, but I prefer to work alone," he grumbled. The last thing he wanted to do now was talk shop.

"I know you do, but I need to have others know what to do in case I have you working on something else." Roman placed the empty glass on a nearby table.

"Speaking of working on something else, I noticed you dancing with Steph." Madison grinned.

"I don't dance." He tried to deny it but her smile got bigger. "I just wanted to talk to her about something."

"Anything we need to be concerned about?" Roman wanted to know everything that was going on in town. If he didn't tell him, someone else would.

"When I dropped off Jasper today, I noticed a biker coming out the back door of the building where she lives. He wasn't a local. I was going to ask her if she knew who it was." Their relationship was strictly business, at least that was what he wanted others to think.

"Did you get plate numbers?" Roman inquired. "After the hit and run a couple months ago, we can't be too careful."

"Yeah, I sent a text to the tech guys but haven't heard back yet."

"Is something going on?" Madison wrapped her arms around Roman's waist. "Do we need to be concerned about Stephanie?"

Roman touched his finger to her chin. "Nothing to worry about. You know I like to keep tabs on everyone. But just to be on the safe side, Dom, I want you to make sure she gets home safe, and let me know as soon as you hear anything on those plates."

"Yes, sir." They may have been around the same age, but Roman was still his boss and demanded respect. He'd also just given him an excuse to stick close to Stephanie. That was a job he wouldn't mind doing.

"Good night, Dominic," the couple added before leaving for the night.

He spied Steph carrying a tray full of empty glasses and quickly hurried to her side. "Why are you doing this? They have busboys."

"What? I told you I have to make sure everything is cleared out before I can go." She placed the tray on the table and went to pick up more glasses. "Why do you want to know anyway?"

"Because you're coming home with me."

"What?" A glass spilled onto the table.

Chapter Four

Stephanie

"I'm what?" She shook her head to clear the noise. The music had been so loud all night that her ears were ringing. Surely she didn't hear him right.

"I'm to see you home. Roman's orders." He tugged at his collar. At least she wasn't the only one overheating. It was hard to concentrate when he was near. That was one of the reasons she'd stayed away for so long.

"Well, good thing I don't have to follow Roman's orders." She righted the glass she'd knocked over and placed it on the tray with the rest.

"Everyone does Roman's bidding." Dominic grabbed an empty tray and started to help with the cleanup.

"Why?" Her face paled.

"Why what?"

"Why do you have to see me home? Not that I'm complaining. It's been a little scary ever since the light in front of the building burned out. I swear the super never fixes anything." She handed her full tray to a passing busboy.

"How long's it been out?" He finished stacking his tray and crossed his arms in front of his chest.

"At least two weeks, but I'm usually home before it gets dark. I just happened to notice when I worked late at the art center one night." She fidgeted as she talked and finally grabbed and folded the tablecloth.

It was a good bet that first thing tomorrow Dom would be there to replace the light and install new locks on her door. That was the way Roman and his men worked. They never liked to wait around for others to do things when they could take care of it themselves. No matter what it was.

"I saw a biker with California plates parked out back of your place," he said quietly.

"You did? When?" Recently, she'd heard a bike come in late at night but was too tired to care. Her car and apartment were in the front so she never had reason to look around back. Living in a place like she did, she'd learned to steer clear of her neighbors. They probably had more to hide than she did.

"I had to drop off Jasper today and I saw the guy." He placed both hands on the table and a strand of his long hair came loose from the messy bun. She had to calm the urge to reach out and push it behind his ear. For a self-proclaimed misfit of society, he was sexy as hell.

"Jasper lives near me?" There were more and more of Roman's "family" members moving to town every day it seemed. Soon, the whole town would be overrun by Mafiosi.

"Close enough." Dom stopped and looked her straight in the eye. "I drive by sometimes to make sure you're okay." His gaze dropped to the floor before returning to hers. "You know. To check and make sure they haven't come back."

The fact that someone cared touched her like never before. She'd made a home here and the last thing she wanted was for the ones looking for her to come to Genoa. Just the thought of it made the room swim before her eyes and he reached out to steady her.

"Sit down." He pulled out a chair.

As much as she tried to push it out of her mind, it was no use. She had nightmares. Nightmares about what happened years ago and also about what happened a couple months ago. Stephanie fidgeted with her bracelets and held one charm between her finger and thumb. The metal warmed to her touch.

Dominic went for her hand but she pulled away. Now was not the time to break down or call attention to herself. She needed to concentrate on getting the place cleaned up and fast. Most of the guests had gone and the band was packing up. She nearly jumped out of her skin when the drummer dropped one of his cymbals.

"Don't worry," he reassured her.

"How can you say that after what we did?" Not only did she have to worry about the motorcycle gang coming after her but about potentially going to jail. They'd killed someone! Well, Dominic did, but she'd told him to. That made her an accessory to murder, even if it was self-defense. They could have let him go and called the cops. The problem was that the guy would have come back and probably brought more criminals with him.

"It was self-defense. You didn't have a choice. If we'd let him go, is there any doubt he would have returned with reinforcements?" Dominic voiced her thoughts out loud.

"No, but we didn't call the police after the fact. Did we?" This time, it was Stephanie who crossed her arms.

"Some things are best left to others. The police would have contacted next of kin and there would have been an investigation. I've never asked who that guy was. Would you rather have told them?"

"No, of course not." Suddenly, the air in the room got heavy. Her shoulders slumped. It was more than fatigue from the long day. She was worn out. The years of hiding had taken their toll. How did one take a vacation from their life?

She rested her head on her fist and tried to ignore the hustle and bustle of everyone rushing around her. She should have been just as busy, but right now, all she could do was sit. Maybe it was time to tell Roman, or Dominic, the truth, but not tonight. Stephanie took a deep breath and sat up straight. She could do this, all she needed was some rest and time to write. Putting things down on paper made it seem like it was just a story, something that had happened to someone else.

"Miss Barclay, we have everything put away and the dishes in the dishwasher. Just have to finish sweeping the dance floor and vacuuming the carpet, and we'll be done." Janey, one of the waitstaff, now stood by their table. "Is there anything else we need to do before we go?"

"No, I will just wait for the band to leave and then lock up. Roman is sending someone for the gifts in the morning. You can go as soon as you're done, and thanks for a great job this evening."

Janey nodded and nervously glanced at Dominic. "Do you need me to wait with you? I can stay and help close."

"No, I'm good. Thanks for asking." Stephanie got to her feet.

"Okay. Well, I'll be here another ten minutes if you change your mind." The young woman stood her ground.

Stephanie placed a hand on her shoulder. "Thanks, but Dominic will see me out so I'll be fine. Have a good night."

"Thanks. You too." Janey's face lit up. "I have a date so I'd better hurry."

"This late at night?" Oh, to be twenty again and be able to stay up all night long. She was twenty-five herself, but some days she felt seventy-five.

"Yeah, we're meeting for drinks at the Pier." It was a nice place on the lakeshore. The Pier had tables and chairs out on the sand for their guests. It would be a great night to sit by the water and gaze at the stars. Janey was giddy and it darkened Stephanie's mood even more.

"Well, have fun and be careful." Just thinking about the guy who might be out searching for her had Stephanie wishing she could lock up and keep safe all the women in town. It wasn't that long ago that a serial killer had been on the loose. Ryan saved Valentina from being the next victim. People were still locking their doors and looking over their shoulders.

"Don't worry, I will." Janey wiggled her fingers goodbye and hurried to the kitchen.

"How much longer?" Dominic's deep voice hummed next to her ear. His breath tickled the nape of her neck. She didn't usually wear her hair up and she quickly covered her tattoo with her hand and turned to face him.

"About fifteen minutes. Will that work?" She said it more gruffly than intended.

"Fine. I'll wait by the bar," he grumbled and marched off.

Guilt knotted in her gut. How could she treat him that way when all he'd ever done was help? She took a step to follow but was interrupted. "We've got everything loaded. Thanks for the gig. See you next time," the manager of the band said as he passed by. He had an extension cord coiled between his hand and his elbow. "I left more business cards up front also."

"Thanks. Great job." She waved and took one more look around. Janey started to turn the lights off and section by section the place went dark. Soon, the place was empty except for by the bar. Stephanie stopped by the kitchen next. A cleaning crew would be there in the morning but it was pretty well picked up for the night. She flicked the light switch and the exit light cast a red glow on the stainless steel appliances. With a frown, she turned around and headed back out into the ballroom. Someone grabbed her arm and her heart stopped.

"Ready?" It was Dominic.

"Jeez, you scared me half to death." She placed a hand on her chest and leaned against the wall to catch her breath.

"Everyone's gone. We should go," he said impatiently. The guy was probably just as tired as she was after the long day and yet he stayed to see her safely home. It wasn't his fault she was in this situation.

"I just need to grab my purse. It's in the office." Their shoes echoed on the tile as he followed her down the hallway to the back offices. She shivered and rubbed her arms. Now that everyone had left, her summer dress was chilly. Searching in her handbag, she found her keys. She couldn't wait to get home and out of her dress shoes. What a relief it would be to finally wiggle her bare toes in the thick rug next to her bed.

Dominic waited and then accompanied her to the front door. He held it open for her as she set the alarm and locked up. The cool lake breeze made her shiver and she rushed to her car. As Stephanie unlocked her door, she was enveloped in a warm coat. Dominic had dropped his suit jacket around her shoulders and she turned to refuse. For so long she'd relied on herself. It would be too easy to get used to the comforts of others.

"Keep it. Do you want me to drive?" He'd let his hair down and it blew in the light wind.

"No, I'm fine, and you really don't need to follow me home."

Dominic started to disagree but she stopped him with a touch to his arm. "But I'm glad you are.

Thank you."

He just nodded and glanced at her backseat. The guy never overlooked anything. If there had been anyone hiding back there, they'd be mincemeat in no time at all. The touchy, warm feeling she'd felt back in the building whenever he was near returned. He may have scared others, but he thrilled her, made her feel alive for the first time in a long time. Dom knew she had secrets but accepted her anyway. He made her feel safe. He was also a loner just like her. Someone she could never have, not that she had any interest in a long-term relationship. Everyone knew Dominic Scarlatti was a lone wolf and a recluse. His loyalty was to the Caponellis and no one else.

The man waited until she was in the car and then headed to his truck. She drove slowly down the street to her place and parked in the closest spot. It was darker than normal out front and just the thought of going in alone sent a chill down her spine. Dominic had kept driving and she frowned. He'd done his job and seen her to her place, but now she had to go in alone. Unconsciously, she pulled the jacket tighter and his outdoorsy scent of pine and some spicy cologne encircled her. In the dark, her apartment building looked like something out of a slasher movie, but it was home. She could do this. She had to unless she planned on sleeping in her car.

Stephanie gripped her keys in one hand and her keychain of mace in the other. Cautiously, she opened the car door and studied her surroundings. All was quiet, except for the sound of heavy footsteps coming down the sidewalk. She tightened her hold on the keys and her finger hovered over the mace trigger.

The footsteps came closer and her grip loosened when Dominic came into view.

"I thought you left." She walked toward the building.

"I had to park my truck down the street." He took the keys from her hand and unlocked her building's front door.

"Why?" She handed him his coat back and he slipped it on.

Dom stepped into her apartment lobby and flipped the light switch. "Because I didn't think you would want everyone to think I spent the night in your place."

"Why would they think that?"

"Because that's what I'm going to do."

Chapter Five

Dominic

Stephanie's mouth dropped open and her eyes grew huge. He had no intention of staying the night but he'd done it to throw her off balance. To give her something else to think about instead of the fear she'd shown ever since he mentioned the biker.

He rubbed the back of his hand against his chin. Who was he kidding? He really wanted to see if she would object. The green-eyed blonde had taken root in his thoughts from the moment they'd first met. It was just last summer that he'd gone to Madison's bridal shop of all places to fix up the mess left behind when a maniac trashed her store. Dresses were slashed, beads and veils were thrown everywhere.

The bastard had smashed a display cabinet and glass had gone flying. A shard had embedded in Stephanie's cheek. He still remembered Roman commenting on how she'd refused to go to the hospital but instead sought care from the "family" doctor. Now he knew the reason why. Hospitals asked questions and wanted personal information. That was something that she wouldn't share.

The mystery surrounding her just intrigued him more, but her quivering lip made him pause. The woman had many things to worry about and he didn't need to add to her stress. She may have a past, but he was not a part of her future. No decent woman would be able to forget or forgive everything he'd done in his life. No decent woman would be able to live the life he did.

"I meant that I am staying until I make sure you're safe. I need to check out the back too." It was really dark out front and in the morning he'd be sure to fix that damn light. The bulb had probably just burned out but it still wasn't good.

Stephanie lived in an older style apartment building. At least the front door locked, and then once inside, each apartment had its own secure door. He followed Stephanie up the stairs. It was hard to not appreciate the view from behind. She had nice long legs and a round ass. Just the way he liked them. Her skirt swayed with each step.

The stairs creaked as they climbed. At the top, a heavy ammonia smell filled the air. "Do they allow pets here?" It stunk like cat piss.

"Uh, no. Not that I know of." Her voice echoed in the hallway. "It's probably the only thing they don't allow, but only because the owner's afraid of dogs and hates cats."

"It burns your nose." Even his eyes watered.

"I think it's some kind of disinfectant or something. I've just noticed it the last few days."

She stopped in front of the door at the end of the hallway.

He cringed at the sight of it. One easy kick by the doorknob and it would easily open. Granted, crime in Genoa was pretty rare, but the thought of her staying here alone didn't sit well. The walls were so thin, he could hear the laughter from some late night talk show playing in the next room.

"What's wrong?" Stephanie brought him out of his thoughts.

"You shouldn't be living here." This place was a dump and a fire hazard.

She set her fists on her hips. "And why not?"

"It's not safe." He fidgeted with her keys until she grabbed his hand and pointed at the right one. Her fingers were like ice.

"I've lived here a long time and nothing's ever happened." She stepped back and rubbed her arms with her hands.

He knew for a fact that Madison had encouraged her friend several times to get a new place, but she'd always turned her down. Money was always the excuse but he knew it was the same reason she hadn't wanted to go to the doctor. It was the paper trail. The owners of this place took cash and didn't ask any questions.

Dominic shed his jacket and draped it around her shoulders again. He expected her to throw it back at him but Stephanie pulled it tighter. She was a tall girl but it still dwarfed her. Someone opened the front door downstairs and her eyes met his. Neither wanted to see who it was as loud boots started up the steps.

Dom stuck the key in the lock and opened the door. With a gentle hand to her back, he ushered her in and flipped the light switch. Stephanie walked over to the plain tan La-Z-Boy, took a seat, and yawned. "Any idea who that was?" He motioned to the door.

"No, and I don't want to know. People come and go. A lot of them work nights so it isn't surprising to hear doors open and close this late." The last few words were slurred.

Stephanie must be exhausted. He had no idea what time she started her day but he'd heard Madison mention that Steph had been at the rehearsal dinner last night, then she'd helped set up some things for the reception before going back to work at the bridal store. Valentina wasn't the only one who had a wedding today and the poor girl was working overtime to keep up with everything.

"I'm going to check your windows. Is this your only door out?"

All she did was nod and even that seemed to take effort. Just minutes ago she'd been ready for a fight, and now she seemed to be fading fast. Her eyes closed as he walked over to the windows. Damn, they had no locks and no fire escape either. How in the hell did this place passcode? What if there was a fire? They were only on the second floor but a fall from that distance would still do some damage. *Son of a bitch.* Dominic pushed a strand of hair behind his ear and shook his head. He didn't like this one damn bit.

Leaning against the windowsill, he surveyed the room. Something just didn't fit. It was a studio type apartment where everything was in one room with the exception of the bathroom and what looked to be a closet. Stephanie had lived here for how many years and yet it was pretty much empty. The kitchen was sparse. Over the counter, cabinets showed only a few dishes, some cans, and a round container of oatmeal. A small coffee maker, toaster, and microwave were the only things on the counter. Obviously, Stephanie's coffee making skills were better than Valentina's as she had a real coffee maker and not a single cup one. Valentina could kill a person with that java junk she served.

The closet door was open and there were very few clothes in there. The bathroom was bare also. A few cosmetics and a toothbrush lay by the sink from what he could see in the small space. The only area in the whole apartment that even looked lived in was in the corner. There sat a desk with piles of books, notepads, and a laptop. He remembered hearing that Stephanie wanted to be a writer but had no clue what that was about. She had some framed poems at the art center but he'd never bothered to read them.

Glancing back where she sat, he noticed she was out like the bulb out front. Her chest gently rose and fell with each breath. It was nice to see her at peace and not ready to jump out of her skin. Ever since what happened that night in the bridal store two months ago, she'd changed. Before that, whenever he'd seen her, Stephanie had just appeared shy or timid. But now she'd turned from timid to terrified. Nearly jumping out of her skin at times, except for when she was working, like tonight, and then the woman was all business.

Stephanie still had his jacket wrapped around her shoulders. Spying a nearby blanket, he draped it over her lap and legs. Even though it was stuffy in the room, the humidity made it damp and he didn't want her to get a chill. With her keys in hand, he left her apartment to check out the rest of the building. There was a back stairway so that was the first place he was going to head. Dominic stepped lightly but it was doubtful anyone would hear him over the loud television sounding from the apartment at the top of the stairs.

The horrible smell was worse in the back. He couldn't put his finger on it but that was no cleaning smell. It was something else. Tomorrow, he would check with Roman about anything illegal going on in this place. Surprisingly, the rear parking lot of the building was brightly lit. There were a few cars, one pickup truck, an old-style van, and back by the trees was a motorcycle. Bikers would never park their bikes under a tree because of bird shit, sap, and leaves, but this one was covered.

Letting his eyes adjust to the bright light, he looked around to see if anyone was in view, but all was quiet. Dominic slowly approached the bike and lifted the tarp. It was a high-end crotch rocket. Way out of the price range of anyone he would expect to live in this apartment complex. He pulled out his phone and lit up the license plate. Quickly snapping a picture of the numbers, he then put the tarp back in place. The number of the other plate he snapped before escaped him but this one was in-state. He rubbed his chin. Nothing seemed to add up right.

Using her key, Dominic slipped back into the building. He sneaked a quick look in the downstairs laundry room, and then stopped by the tenants' mailboxes, hoping to find some names on the plaques. Nothing. A few had a first initial and last name, but very few. Nothing stood out as odd.

He hadn't planned on staying the night, but after seeing this place, it just didn't seem right to leave. What if something happened that he could have prevented? Guilt kicked in. Was he just trying to convince himself he needed to remain? Stephanie never fussed about living there that he knew of. The woman never complained and never freaked out over the bad things that happened to her. She was stronger than everyone thought and he admired that.

Dom took the stairs, careful to step closest to the wall where the steps were strongest and not likely to make as much noise. His eyes burned at the top.

"Dammit, what is that fucking smell?" He should know it, but for some reason, he just couldn't think. Probably because his main concern was Stephanie. Someone had to look out for her. Her vulnerability in the world spoke to him like nothing ever had. The urge to keep her safe came out of nowhere and sucker punched him in the gut.

Walking past the door with the loud television, the only thing that stopped him from putting a fist through the wall and telling them to shut the damn thing off was that he knew it would wake the sleeping beauty down the hall. Since when did he care what others thought? He still didn't, he just wanted her to get some much-needed sleep.

Quietly as he could, Dominic entered her

apartment again. She slept soundly. It was a done deal—he would stay until the morning and then slip away before she woke. It was late, so it'd only be a few more hours. He eyed her desk again. There was a bookshelf behind it, and he did like to read. After removing his boots, he wandered over to the desk.

Judging by the titles, they were all romance books. Was that what she wrote? On the wall by the shelf was a bulletin board with *Heroes and Heroines* across the top. There were various photos of handsome men and beautiful women that must be the inspiration for the characters in her stories. Some had names under them or notes. He turned toward the books again and then did a double take back to the board. Dominic leaned in. *What in the hell?* Right in the middle of the board was a picture of him.

Chapter Six

Stephanie

In April, she'd hit a biker with her car—on purpose. That wasn't what she'd set out to do that fine spring morning. No, it was a simple coffee run to the Genoa Java Shop with Madison. When they'd left the parking lot, the guy came out of nowhere. A bad dream from her past that'd come to life. Once she saw who it was, her foot automatically hit the gas, not the brake.

After they came to a screeching halt, Madison was shocked, to say the least, when Stephanie asked her to stay and take the blame right before running off. When Roman and Dominic arrived soon after, they knew immediately that Madison hadn't been driving. Heck, it was Stephanie's vehicle. Her purse and the coffee cup with her name on it were still inside.

That same night, Dominic showed up to escort her to Firenza to be questioned by Roman. The man was furious that someone would blame his wife for something she didn't do. When they questioned her, she blew it off and blamed it on having lost her license, but they knew something was up, just not what it was. No one knew that one of the men who had turned her life into a nightmare was here, in Genoa of all places. So scared was she that Dom took her home to his place and she went willingly.

It was a stormy night, and he'd kept her calm when her nerves were ready to shatter. How she used to love a good thunderstorm, but ever since that night all those years ago, the flashes of lightning and loud claps of thunder caused a flood of bad memories to come rushing back, memories of betrayal, unspeakable crime, and now murder. None of it was really her fault but it felt like it. One couldn't choose the family they were born into, but they could do their best to escape them.

She stirred in the chair and then snuggled back into the warmth of the jacket surrounding her. It smelled like pine, fresh air, and a little bit of wood smoke. The scents were comforting. It was like coming home to a safe place. They reminded her of Dominic. What a contradiction that was. He would never be considered "safe."

The man represented everything she hated. He was Mafioso, he was a killer, and he was a cleaner for the mob. If anyone was a picture of evil, it was him. But what a pretty picture he was. It was like two sides of a very different coin. One shiny and new while the other was tarnished and older than the date stamped on it.

His face flashed in her mind. The man was tall with an athletic build, not bulky like Arlo. He had deep brown eyes that never seemed to miss anything and a perfectly straight nose. His strong jaw was usually covered by a beard or goatee. It was like he'd stepped out of the pages of some historical fantasy book. Just picturing him in pirate attire and standing on a ship caused her to moan out loud, but it was his long dark hair that intrigued her the most.

Whether he wore it down or tied up in the back, the man was sexy as hell. Stephanie shifted again in the chair. He was all wrong for her, for any woman. How did one get past what he did? Yet he took care of her when no one else had and protected her without asking why. She would have died if he hadn't arrived at the right time. She shivered and pushed it out of her head. What did she really think of the man?

Stephanie was covered in a blanket and the scent of pine was fresh in her nose. Her eyes fluttered and closed. Dom was there and he pulled the jacket tighter around her shoulders. It should have jolted her awake yet it felt nice to know he was there and that she'd have someone looking out for her for once. Her skin warmed and she snuggled deeper into the chair. Fatigue was getting the best of her as she slipped in and out of sleep. Maybe just one time she could get a full night's sleep without waking in a cold sweat.

Yet in her slumber, she dreamed of a good man who was a bad man. Dominic was a man with as many wounds and inner scars as she. One time, Madison mentioned that she'd suggested to Roman that they try to fix the two of them up. Roman's only response was that Dominic was a loner and had "issues." He didn't elaborate further, yet Maddy and Valentina didn't shy away from encouraging the two even though neither had acted on it.

What did it matter? If her enemies found her, she'd be on the lam again anyway. Running for her life couldn't be called living. Fear resurfaced and sleep started to flee. Stephanie stretched and rubbed her eyes. Oh, how she needed rest and yearned for a peaceful sleep. She blinked a couple times and searched the room. Had Dominic left? No. He was in the corner of the room by her desk. He'd bent over to study her board, her inspiration board.

Oh no. Her eyes widened and then closed. He'd seen the photo, that was for sure. How could anyone miss it? Even if she couldn't sleep, she would pretend to. There was no way she could explain his face showing up in a collage of handsome hunks. Stephanie spent her downtime reading and writing stories of love and happily-ever-afters. Even if that wasn't in the cards for her, she could live it through the pages of a novel.

But why had she put his photo there? He scared her, repulsed her…intrigued her. At least that was what she tried to convince herself of. Sure, he was darker than night, but there was still light in him. She'd seen it when no one else cared to look, but he was still a mystery. It was her belief that deep down he was a good man with a good heart, but no one ever really knew another. Stephanie should be shaking in the chair, but for some reason, she remained calm. There were worse things and scarier people, that was for sure. Still, she needed to keep her distance. She would keep things civil and nothing more. For now, anyway.

The floor creaked. He was coming her way. Her heart should be pounding but exhaustion had taken over. She couldn't raise her head if she wanted to. Stephanie sighed and fell asleep.

***

She woke with a start. A door slammed somewhere down the hall and then loud feet sounded on the stairs. It was a Sunday morning. Did someone have to go to work and they angrily wished to wake everyone else as well?

Stephanie rubbed her eyes and yawned. She was on the couch. Her gaze wandered back to the chair she'd fallen asleep in. Try as she might, she had no idea how she ended up on the Davenport. The jacket fell from her shoulders and the scent of pine drifted to her nose. *Dominic!* She bolted straight up. Her bare toes dug into the fuzzy rug on the floor.

The man was nowhere to be found. She took a deep breath. Sometime during the night, he must have carried her over to where she now lay. At least she didn't have to explain his placement on her wall. The smell of freshly brewed coffee was in the air. Just the thought of it helped clear the cobwebs from her head. After a quick trip to the bathroom, she slipped on a pair of flip-flops and headed to the kitchen area.

The timer had been set and coffee was brewing. Even though it was warm in the room, she pulled his jacket tightly around her body once again.

Stephanie never used the timer on the machine so he must have done it for her before he left. She wandered to the window. His truck was parked across the street.

Even from that distance, she could see him watching the building and its surrounding area. His face turned in her direction and she dropped the shade. The man was watching her, concerned for her. Both sent a chill down the back of her neck. Carefully, she pushed the shade back and rested her forehead on the cool glass. Her heart sank. His truck was now gone.

She reached for her hair and twirled a strand around one finger, tying it in a knot, then two. What had she been expecting? Him asking her to Sunday brunch? No, they both liked to skirt the edge of society. But still…

Tossing his jacket over the back of the chair, Stephanie poured a cup of coffee. It was strong, just like the man who made it. Shaking her head, she put the mug back on the counter. It was time to get out of this place before she went crazy. It was time for a run. She slipped out of her dress and into a tank top, shorts, and running shoes. Grabbing her car keys, a water bottle, and her backpack, she headed out the door.

The place was quiet. She hesitated by the stairs, wondering if she should look out back for the motorcycle Dom mentioned, but the fact that he left made it seem like the danger was over. She skipped down the stairs and out the door. It was muggy for so early in the day. A chance of rain was in the forecast for later.

This was the best time of year. Everything was lush green and full of life. When she ran along the walking path that surrounded the lake, Stephanie usually took the side where Madison lived as it was more open. But today she decided to take the more wooded path by Black Point Estate. The local boat company took visitors there once a day for tours of the old historical mansion. Valentina and Ryan had gone there on their first date. Surprisingly, Stephanie had never been.

There were several parking lots where walkers and joggers could leave their cars and she pulled into the nearest one. The sun was bright and hot, so it would be nice to run on the shady side of the lake. She slipped on her sunglasses, headphones, and stuffed her water bottle, keys, and phone into the small backpack. Looping the straps over her shoulders, she put her hair up in a ponytail, stretched, and started her run.

The rumble of a boat motor started up and she watched as one the famous Lake Genoa wooden boats eased away from the dock and out onto the lake. The driver sported a big cigar in his mouth and there were a few fishing poles poking up in the back. He nodded in her direction and she waved back.

After the first mile, she hit her stride. Her legs had loosened up and it felt good to be running up and down the small hills. She breathed in the fresh air of the surrounding pines. A reminder of someone she was trying to forget. Her strive for fitness wasn't just to stay in shape, it was to survive. If someone were to chase her, they would have a hard time keeping up.

The song she was listening to ended and she heard the snap of a branch. She lost her footing and nearly stumbled. As much as she liked the coolness and quiet of this area, it was also out of the view of homes and most of the lake. Another snap sounded. Stephanie peeked behind her and glimpsed feet. She lengthened her stride. Black Point Estate was up ahead somewhere, maybe another half mile or so. Tour guides might be there waiting on the trail for the arrival of the next tour.

The runner closed in and she gave it all she had. She shouldn't be paranoid, but after what Dominic said last night, she was. Her heart pounded and she breathed through her mouth. So much for going on a run in the hopes of relieving some pent-up tension. She was far from relaxed. Stephanie was in a full-blown panic and afraid to even turn around. Though for all she knew, it could just be some kid from the local track team.

The crow's nest at the top of the historic house came into view. It wouldn't be long before she reached the estate, and hopefully, some of the volunteers would be outside. Someone called out but she kept going. One of her earbuds fell out and bounced against her chest. Just a few more steps and she would be safe.

Out of nowhere, a hand reached out and grabbed her arm. Acting on instinct, she turned and did a kick toward the man's chest. Before she knew it, her foot was in his hands and she was falling. Her butt hit the rocky ground. Hard. Stephanie flipped the hair out of her face and looked up at her attacker.

Deep brown eyes stared back. It was Dominic, and boy did he look angry.

Chapter Seven

"What the hell are you doing running out here? Alone." He still held her foot up in the air. His eyes glared into hers. Sharp rocks poked her behind. They would definitely be leaving a mark.

"I'm getting some exercise." She jerked her leg but he wouldn't let go. "What does it look like I'm doing?"

"It looks like you are taking stupid chances with your life." He leaned down.

That great hair of his was up in the back but a few strands hung loose. She debated on whether to slap his face or caress his cheek. The intensity on his face warmed her from the inside out. Dominic wore shorts, tennis shoes, and a sleeveless tee. He was the most casual dresser of all of Roman's crew. Dom seemed to go by his own set of rules; he was the mob's own version of a rebel without any cause but his own. No designer suits for him. At least she'd never seen him in one.

"I'm perfectly capable of taking care of myself. I've been doing it for years."

He rolled his eyes, tugged on her foot, and smirked.

"Would you let go of my leg?" She pulled back but he held tight.

"Until we know why the guys, whoever the fuck they are, are really here, you need to be careful and stay out of sight."

"I agree. That's one of the reasons I am running on this side of the lake." She motioned to the trees above. "I can't be seen here."

"I found you. And what's with the earphones? How are you supposed to hear if someone is following you?"

He had her there and she pouted. "I know, that was stupid. It won't happen again. I saw you leave this morning so figured it was safe."

"I had to get out of those damn wedding clothes and get us some breakfast. Ever hear of grocery shopping? A person would starve at your place."

"You looked in my fridge?" she yelled. The nerve of the guy invading her privacy. The last thing she wanted was someone poking around in her business.

"I was hungry and thought I'd make us something to eat, like eggs or bacon, but I couldn't even find bread to make toast."

Her ire softened a bit when he mentioned cooking for her. Still, it was best to stay as far away from Dominic Scarlatti as possible. For her own sake and his.

She rubbed the back of her hand across her forehead and then rested it on the ground. The dirt was soft, cool, and pine needles stuck to her palm.

"So, did you get anything?" Stephanie turned her face up toward his.

"Get what?"

"Food." Her stomach growled.

"When I got back, I saw your car was gone so I went looking for you. Lucky for you, I spotted your car. You know, the car with fake plates and registration that we had to fix for you?" It was true. After the accident with the motorcycle, Ryan demanded Roman get everything up to snuff so he didn't have to fill out a report.

"Yeah, lucky me." Stephanie ground the heel of her loose foot into the ground and struggled to get the other one free from his grasp. "Are you ever going to let go of my foot?"

"Make me." His eyes narrowed.

"Why are you doing this?" She was hungry, tired, and all the blood from her leg being in the air was starting to rush to her head.

"You may have bad guys after you." The grip on her ankle tightened. "Consider this a learning moment."

She'd teach him. Her fingers dug into the loose dirt. Steph glanced behind him and her eyes widened. "Oh no. Who's that?"

Dominic twisted to look but there was nothing there. When he turned back, she threw the handful of dirt in his face and scooted back. It didn't work. He still held tight. Damn.

A smile crossed his mouth as he wiped the dust from his face with his forearm. "Good try, but even an idiot would be expecting that."

"I made you look," she sneered.

"Are you free yet?" he teased.

It was of no use. He was bigger than her and wasn't letting go.

"I give up." She raised her hands. "Would you please let go of my foot?"

"Nope." He squatted in front of her. If it weren't for the trees, he would be her shade now. His hand moved to her calf. "You have nice legs. Such soft skin." His voice lowered and her heart pounded. "Are you really going to do nothing?" He arched an eyebrow. "What if I moved my hand to your thigh?" His hand inched higher up her leg. She froze. Was this still part of the test? She swallowed and goosebumps rose on her skin.

"You're breathing hard. Is it the run or me?" The man was teasing her, testing her. There was no denying that. That pine scent that she always associated with him flooded her senses.

She couldn't move. If someone she'd feared had a hold of her, she'd be fighting tooth and nail, but right now, she remained motionless. His gaze was intense and intoxicating.

"Are you drawing me closer so you can attack?" he whispered near her ear.

"Maybe," she choked out. Who could think when he was this close? When she could feel his breath on her skin.

"You should be." He sat back and narrowed his eyes.

Stephanie shook her head. "What? I don't get…" The man confused her. What was she supposed to do? He wasn't the enemy. "I don't want to fight you. You're twice my size. I couldn't win for anything."

"If you find yourself in a bad situation with someone bigger than you, go for the throat. Even a small woman can take down a huge man if she punches him there." He dropped her leg and it thumped on the ground. Dom stood and held a hand out to her.

The bastard. She ignored the outstretched hand and rose by herself. Punch someone in the throat? That's exactly what she wanted to do right now. She was enthralled by his good looks and he was trying to give self-defense pointers. What a fool she was.

Stephanie turned her back to him and started walking. Her thoughts were scrambled. Had it been so long since a man had given her any attention that she was practically begging for someone's touch? Or did she just seem to crave the wrong kind of guy?

"Hey? Where are you going?" he called out to her.

"Away from you." She walked faster. "Touch me again and I'll do more than punch your throat." The man mystified her and she needed space.

His footsteps stirred the pebbles on the walk behind her but she didn't stop. Finally, the stairs to Black Pointe Estate came into view. There were no guides in sight but she made the climb anyway. It was a long way up, at least a hundred steps. Stephanie could feel his presence behind her but still wouldn't acknowledge him. At least he seemed to respect her need for space.

She took a moment to catch her breath at the top and then wandered over to the fountain. The bubbling water calmed her nerves a bit. What if it had been someone from her past who had tackled her on the trail? Instead of standing here, she might be in the trunk of a car right now going god knew where. It was time to stay sharp, not be sharp. Whatever the reason for Dominic trying to help her, now was not the time to turn it down. If the ones who sought her showed up, she wanted to be prepared.

A breeze gently blew the branches of the trees. It was said that the original owner planted a ton of different kinds of elms. Flowers were everywhere and their fragrance and colors attracted singing birds and buzzing bees. She glanced at the lake. The view was breathtaking. Lake Genoa was truly home now and there was no way she wanted to leave. She was tired of looking over her shoulder and living in fear.

Stephanie tapped the concrete fountain base with her running shoes. Memories floated back from April. She had just closed up the bridal store when the man she'd hit with her car, Handlebar, showed up. He was going to give her up. Stephanie fought for her life and would have died if Dominic hadn't shown up. With the guy struggling in his hold, Dom asked her if she wanted the man dead. She didn't think twice about it then and would do it again now. Her answer was yes. She was in survival mode at the time but it'd given her nightmares ever since.

After Dom saved her and made the mess go away, he'd returned to make sure she was all right. She owed him for what he did and he said he would collect. That had made her heart drop. No one wanted to be indebted to the mob, but this was something different. This was worse. Dominic had gone against Roman's orders by killing the man. Roman hadn't known that the biker had returned and threatened to expose her. He'd gone against his boss to protect her.

The man should have been furious with her, but instead of blaming her, something else happened— the kiss of a lifetime. A kiss that sent her soaring to the heavens and had her going to sleep with a smile on her face every night since. That was the last thing she expected from him. Not that he wouldn't be a great kisser, the man was sexy as hell. She just didn't think he would ever turn his attention to her. It was the best kiss of her life.

But what did he really mean by saying she owed him and that he would be collecting? So far, he'd asked for nothing, giving her many sleepless nights. He'd followed her up the stairs. She took a peek behind her, in his direction. Did he want money? Companionship? Sex? A new toy to play with and then toss aside? It was anyone's guess as he'd never come to collect. It'd been in the back of her mind ever since that he would show up at her door some night demanding payment, but he never did. He'd kept his distance. Until now.

Dominic had killed for her. Protected her even now. It was time that she stood up for herself and stopped running. If they came here, she would be ready. It was time to fight back and he was going to help her. She'd left one home and family already. There was no way she'd lose another.

She stretched and arched her back. It was hard

not to notice when his gaze dropped to her breasts. The man wanted her but would probably never admit it. There was no other reason for him to be looking out for her. He would never ask her out, that was for sure. Dominic was not a dating kind of guy and she was not interested in a casual relationship.

She crossed her arms in front of her chest. Peeking over her shoulder, she saw that he now sat on the front steps of the historic house. His elbows rested on his knees. He hadn't deserted her but kept his distance.

Entwining her fingers behind her back, she walked along the brick sidewalk until she stood in front of the porch where he sat.

"I'm sorry for being a bitch. I know you're just trying to help."

He just sat and stared at the lake.

"I have no clue why you are helping me and looking out for me, but I really appreciate it." She took a seat beside him on the stairs. "I was thinking I could use a few more learning moments." That seemed to get a rise out of him and he turned to look her in the face. "Would you teach me how to fight? How to save myself if you aren't around to do it for me?"

He groaned and swore under his breath. This was serious even if she didn't want it to be so. "Yes, I can't always be there."

"I don't expect you to be." She pulled her knees up and wrapped her arms around them.

"You're going to have to do what I say whether you like it or not."

"Yeah, sure." They offered self-defense classes at the police department. This would probably be something similar, only mafia-style. What did she have to lose but her life?

Dominic rose. "How far do you usually run?"

"Couple miles. I usually walk a half mile, run some, and then walk the rest back. I'm not a long-distance runner. I just do it so I can keep eating chocolate and drinking those French vanilla cappuccinos without gaining too much weight." He didn't need to know she did it to outrun anyone who might be chasing her. His gaze dropped to her feet and then slowly lingered on her frame as he took his time getting back to her face. Her skin tingled with the appraisal.

"You're perfect the way you are." His face flushed after he said it. Was he blushing? "But today you run three miles." He turned and took off down the stairs.

"What?" She rushed after him. "What did you say?"

"You heard me." He stopped and she plowed into this back. It was like hitting a warm, hard wall. "Do you know what the best way to keep from getting caught is?" Dom put his hands on his waist. He was a step below and still had to look down at her. Those stunning eyes of his sparkled with mischief.

"Huh?" What was he talking about? It was so easy to get distracted when he was around.

"The best way to keep from getting caught is to run faster and farther than the one chasing you." He took another step down. "You need to up your game, sunshine." She couldn't agree with him more on that but she was exhausted.

"I was up all night and I already ran a mile. Can we start this another time?" She was whining but knew it needed to be done. That was the reason she punished herself.

"Nope." He paused and rested his hand on the white wood railing. "Let's go."

"And if I don't?" Stephanie stood her ground. Her legs were still tired from the run and all the stairs.

"Then I throw you in the lake. Head first." He smiled and kept on going.

Chapter Eight

Dominic

"Why the hell did I suggest this?" Stephanie gave a big sigh from behind him before she went shuffling by. She seemed to thrive on dares and competition.

"Because you want to live," he reminded her. She'd already run a mile but still smelled fresh and clean. What was it about the perfumes that women used that made men want to follow them like wolves on the scent of prey?

There still was no clue to her story or why anyone would want to harm a hair on that beautiful head. It was serious, though, and she needed to be reminded of that every day. He knew all about letting your guard down. That was the moment your enemies swooped in and crushed you. That was the last thing he wanted to see happen to her.

As soon as she hit the bottom stairs, she was off in a flash. He had no doubt the woman had another mile or two left in her but he'd watch for signs of fatigue or if her steps faltered. The last thing he wanted to do was push too hard. Those long, tanned legs of hers were almost out of view when he strolled down the last flight of stairs. Never did he think he would be spending the day chasing after Stephanie Barclay when he'd done his best to run away from her.

Dominic was used to being in the company of gorgeous women. Roman trusted him to guard his wife and his sister. It was a position of honor. Both women were smart and it was a great change from being around morons like Jasper and other young guns trying to move up the ladder fast. Well, maybe Jasper wasn't a total idiot but he was annoying at times. If it wasn't for him, Dom wouldn't have had the chance to dance with Steph. Well, actually, they didn't really dance—dancing was for pussies, he tried to convince himself.

He started jogging slowly, no need to be breathing down Stephanie's neck. She probably needed time to herself. He could tell she liked her privacy just as much as he did. Hell, he should be back at his cabin sharpening knives and working on swords. He'd spent enough time in the company of others in the past twenty-four hours to last him for months.

Dominic covered his mouth as he yawned. Sleep had been pretty much non-existent last night and yesterday had been a long day. He'd had a clean-up with a novice, a wedding, and a young lady to watch over. When had his life gotten so crazy? Crazy might not be the right word. Complicated? Messed up? How about invaded by a blonde, green-eyed little bridal consultant who wrote romance novels on the side?

He shook his head just thinking about it. When he'd heard from Madison that Steph liked to write, he thought maybe poetry or mysteries. The last thing he ever thought of was romance. Steph wasn't exactly someone who was out buying flowers, dating online, or talking about marriage from what he'd heard. It was the opposite. She hid from people and hated any kind of attention. The threat from her past made it clear why she'd been trying to slip under the radar and go through life unnoticed.

Maybe her stories were her way of living out her life the way she wished it could be instead of the way it was. Her eyes were often on the lake, not focusing on where she was going. That was one of the things he would caution her on when they stopped. Her stride had picked up speed and her shoes were now on the paved part of the walking path. They'd gone a quarter mile in no time flat.

His cell buzzed and he stopped to answer. It was the tech guys getting back to him. Dominic had no clue who they were. Everyone just referred to them that way. In this business, no one really wanted to draw attention to what they did. No one was supposed to know he was the cleaner but those closest to the family.

"What have you got?" Dominic answered and turned his back to Stephanie as if shielding her from the call would protect her from harm.

"Sorry it took so long, but with the wedding and everything, we were working overtime checking the guest list." The wedding had kept everyone working overtime. At least it was a small one, but still every vendor, florist, and guest had to be checked and double checked before they could enter the Caponelli home or Firenza.

"Did you find anything?"

"I ran the plates you gave me and then scanned the cameras around town for any additional bikes matching that description. The bike is from California, but that's because the owner purchased it there and had it shipped." The guy gave Dom the owner's name. It was the lead singer of a major rock band who had a house on the lake. Famous people from all over the world had homes there. It was low crime, low profile, and a great place to live the high life out of the view of the press. Heck, the Playboy club used to be on the lake.

"So why did I see it parked in the lot behind an apartment building?"

"Looks like a guy who lives there picked it up for him at the shipping company and then drove it here. Probably just wanted to drive it around a bit to show off before dropping it off with the new owner."

"So, no threat." That was a relief.

"None that I can see as far as the bikes go. Roman has me on another project but I will keep an eye out for anything odd going on. It's tourist season so a lot of new people in town."

"Yeah, thanks. I appreciate it." Dom ended the call and stuck the phone in his pocket.

He turned to see how far Steph had gone. She was at least a half mile ahead.

Stephanie glanced back at him and when she saw

he was almost out of sight, it seemed to spur her to go faster. For a while, she sprinted. Her arms pumping. Her light hair bouncing back and forth as she ran. At least she was in the wide-open spot of the trail and there were houses nearby.

Up ahead, two guys were jogging their way. They were locals, a couple of rich trust fund babies who lived at the lake during the summer. When she caught sight of them, he noticed her steps slow and she detoured toward a public dock. One of the playboys elbowed the other and pointed in her direction. She was a very attractive woman, and as much as she tried to hide, it made her a mark to any red-blooded male, including himself. Dominic watched as they followed her.

The only way off the dock was to go in the water. Another thing he needed to warn her about. Know all possible exits and have a plan of escape no matter the location. When the guys followed her onto the dock, he could see her body stiffen.

Whereas Valentina was all out there with her tight clothes and high heels, Stephanie was more modest and sweeter. For the first time in a long time, Dominic surprised himself. He was a killer who had no business even being in the same room with someone as nice as Steph and yet he was thinking about her in sweet and romantic terms. Women made a man weak and became potential targets. She was way out of his league, but that didn't mean he was going to let some lowlife have her either.

The two men in designer sunglasses that probably cost more than most people made in a month approached Stephanie as she stood at the end of the pier, gazing at the water and stretching. One man was on each side of her and Dom's fists clenched. He shouldn't have let her get so far ahead, but he also wanted to see how she handled herself. He slowed his pace but was ready to jump into action anytime he was needed.

The first dickwad tried to distract her while the other stood behind her, making some obscene gesture toward her ass. Dominic ground his teeth as he waited to see how this played out. At least he was now close enough to hear what they said.

"Yes, we live in the house over there. The really big one. You should stop by for a drink. I bet you're thirsty after running." Polo shirt jerk pointed to their mansion.

"Thanks, but no. I have to get going." She turned and the other guy took her arm.

"What's your hurry, doll?"

"No hurry. Just not interested." Stephanie tried to brush them off but they weren't taking no for an answer. "Let go of my arm."

A twinge of guilt hit Dom after grabbing her leg not too long ago. She'd been manhandled enough for one day and if she didn't do something soon, he would have to step in.

"Or you'll do what?" the jerk who wouldn't let go mocked.

"This." With her free hand, she slugged him in the throat with her fist. While the other man stood there in shock, she kicked out with her foot and nailed him right in the chest. The man landed in the cold lake and the other dropped his hold on her as if she was a hot coal. He fell to his knees, his hand to his neck, and gasped for air.

With her head high, Stephanie walked toward him. Dominic's admiration for her was at a new high, but she looked pissed.

"Did you put them up to that?" She motioned over to where one was struggling to get to his feet while the other flapped around in the water.

He frowned. "Do I look like the kind of person who would hang out with a couple of pricks like that?" That seemed to calm her a bit. "I had no idea you were even going to be here. Remember?"

One of the men yelled at her and waved a fist.

"Let's get the hell out of here." Dominic placed a hand on her lower back. If they bothered her again, they'd have to deal with him. From the dejected looks on their faces, he doubted they would see either one of them again. The one man coughed and still fought to get air. The other finally dragged himself out of the lake.

"I maybe overreacted a bit." Stephanie bit her lip. "Do you suppose we should go help them?"

"Hell, no." He started to jog in the hopes she would follow suit. It worked and she was soon beside him.

"I didn't mean to hurt them. Do you think I broke anything?" Her chin jutted out.

"That's the problem with you women. You don't fight back because you're all too afraid of hurting others. Do you think these bastards would have cared if you scrapped a knee as they dragged you into the bushes?" It was doubtful they were going to do that in broad daylight but one never knew.

She stopped in her tracks. "I think they were just some rich kids looking for company and I overreacted. I'm so embarrassed. I should go back."

"Absolutely not." Dominic faced her and placed a hand on each of her shoulders. "Don't overthink it. Like I said, do you know how many women have been kidnapped without even saying a word?" He choked. "You can't be too careful. Never apologize for being safe."

Her lower lip quivered but she nodded. "Okay."

"You did good and listened to what I told you. You walked away, and that is the most important thing."

She glanced into the distance and then back toward him. "I've had enough for the day. I want to go home." The poor woman did appear tired. Her face had paled and her shoulders were limp.

"Let's jog to Black Point and then we'll walk the rest of the way. Can you make it?" An older couple had stopped to see if the college kids needed help so it was time to get out of their line of sight and fast.

"Yes, I'm fine." She sprinted off, leaving him in the dust again.

He stood there and admired her lean legs and tight ass. Damn, he was as bad as the creeps who just tried to hustle her. Reaching down, he picked up a rock that was lying in the middle of the path. No, he was better than them. He would never lay a hand on any woman against their will. If he touched Stephanie, it was to prove a point or teach her how to get out of a hold. With more force than he intended, Dom vaulted the rock into the lake. Its impact making a loud plunk.

Dominic started running again. The problem was he did want to touch her. Her soft skin drew him like a magnet. Her scent was pure and clean. He was the one who was beneath her and would never be good enough for her. They'd only run a total of maybe two miles but his legs ached. He needed the exercise as much as she did. Up ahead, she stood waiting by the stairs of Black Point. A few older tour guides had started down to wait for the boatload of tourists to arrive.

There was one talking to Stephanie and he recognized her as one of the crafters from the art center. The woman turned her back toward him. It was slight but he'd seen it. The others paid him no mind and just went about their duties. Not wanting to draw attention to himself or her, he kept going. He'd wait up ahead for her. After cresting the hill, he slowed and bent over at the waist. Just a few short minutes later, Stephanie walked toward him.

"Why didn't you stop? You know Carol from the art center." When she was by his side, they started toward the parking lot.

"Didn't feel like it. Besides, I saw her turn her back to me."

"I wish you had. She didn't want the others to hear."

"Hear what?"

"She thinks her grandson might be mixed up in drugs. I told her I thought you could help. I know how Roman feels about drugs in town."

Was that really why she'd turned away? "Where does she think he's getting them?" Roman kept a close eye on things and anyone dealing in the city limits would be relocated fast. No questions asked.

"Not sure, but she thinks near the school."

"Give me the kid's name and I'll get Roman the information."

"I don't want him hurt." She tilted her head.

"We're not going to hurt him. We just want to know where he's getting the drugs. We'll put a tail on him. The kid won't even know anyone's watching."

She let out a deep breath and reached for her phone. "I'll text it to Madison. You know I hate that you guys are in the mafia. But I do feel there are worse people out there."

If she had any idea what his past had been like, she'd know firsthand that Dominic used to be one of them.

Chapter Nine

Stephanie

It felt good to get out of the house, but now that she'd returned to her dingy place her funk was back. Whether it was still the effects of the wedding or the possible threat from the biker in town, it was hard to tell. She needed a break from life and a vacation from reality.

Dominic had followed her home and parked his truck behind her car. Now what? She got out of the car but he hadn't moved. On sore legs, she slowly walked back to where he parked.

"I had the plates of that biker checked out."

She held her breath.

"It belongs to some rock star who lives on the lake."

Stephanie let out a sigh. "So they're not here." She leaned an arm on the roof of his truck. The heat warmed her arm.

"Who?"

She opened her mouth but stopped. He'd almost

caught her, but the less he, and everyone else, knew the better. "Just friends of Handlebar's."

"Members of his club? You ever going to tell me about them?" he grumbled. "Tell me about the man I killed for you?"

It was the least she could do but it wasn't going to happen. Not today anyway. Her shoulders slumped. Slowly, she shook her head.

"Nope." She straightened. "So there's no threat?"

"None that we see at the moment." He ran his fingers through his hair.

"I'm kind of tired. I'm going in." Stephanie turned and headed for the front door of the complex, half expecting him to follow, but he didn't. Surprisingly, disappointment sunk in. When she reached the door, she stopped and twisted around just as he drove off.

"I guess I know where I stand," she mumbled. What did she expect? The man was only trying to keep her safe, and when the threat was gone, he left. He was probably only being nice because of Madison.

Her legs protested as she climbed the stairs. It might be best to do some yoga and stretch. Her lungs were still fresh from the run and that rotten egg smell burned her nose as she reached the top of the stairs.

Someone needed to contact the super about that. What if it was a gas leak? Were the new tenants total pigs and not keeping their kitchen clean? Who knew. Stephanie dragged her fingers along the railing at the top. The air was stagnant in her room so she opened a window. Looking outside, Dominic was nowhere to be seen. She hadn't exactly been kind to him. He scared her but he also seemed to be there whenever she needed him. Tossing her keys on the table, she took a seat in front of her laptop. Firing it up, she checked her messages. It was just the usual junk mail.

Loneliness was something that had been a constant companion for years but it was one that she was getting sick of. Bringing up her documents, she scanned over the last few pages of her work in progress. It was a romance. She usually wrote happy, sappy stories, but her mood had changed in the last few months. Why try to pretend she was something she wasn't? Her life would never be picket fences, roses, and the storybook two point five kids and a dog. Well, maybe a dog.

She typed a few lines but couldn't get into it. People thought it was easy to write. That one just sat down and words fell to the pages like blood flowing from a vein. It didn't work that way. How could she write about love when she had never been in love? She'd been engaged once, but that wasn't her choice. Any feelings she felt for him had been immature and ill-informed.

She set the computer aside. It was no use. Today, everything felt off. Damn that wedding. Working in the bridal store had never bothered her, but today she felt lost. Empty. Like her true love would never find her, she was so well hidden. He was probably out there somewhere looking for her under her real name. It had taken a while to get used to being called Stephanie. It was close to her given name but different enough to cause her to hesitate the first few times someone had called her that.

She rested her chin on her fist and dropped her elbow on the desk. "I'm bored and have no imagination anymore." She spoke out loud to no one. "I'm not inspired anymore." She turned her attention to the board that hung on her wall by the desk. It featured photos of all the characters in her books so she could keep track of what everyone looked like. Things like who had blue eyes and who had brown.

They all left her feeling nothing until her eyes focused on the photo of Dominic. She'd said it before and she'd say it again. The man was an enigma. He was a puzzle with a few of the pieces missing, yet she couldn't stop trying to figure them out. The man made her heart race and her toes tingle.

The tall blacksmith did make her feel. Even before what happened with Handlebar, he'd always intrigued her. Was it because he was a mystery? Someone who lived on the border of quiet society, just like she did? He wasn't someone to bring home to meet the parents. That was for sure. The man did funny things to her stomach whenever he was near. She'd sneakily taken the photo at last year's Snowflake Ball at Firenza. There was a serial killer in town and he was working security at it. Roman wanted no ladies to leave unattended and Valentina insisted that he escort her home.

Nothing had happened. He'd walked her to her car, checked the back seat, and then followed her home. After parking out front, he ensured she made it safely to her apartment and then drove off, just like he had earlier. They'd barely exchanged five words the whole time. It had shocked the hell of her when he came to her rescue after what happened with the biker. She reached out and pulled the photo from the wall. The man was more villain inspiration than hero, yet he kept coming to her aid. A true bad guy wouldn't do that. Even if no one saw it, there was a beating heart under the tough skin. Maybe she wasn't as afraid of him as she thought.

Her stomach growled and she tossed Dominic's picture on the desk. It was after eleven in the morning and she still hadn't eaten. Opening the windows did little to cool the place down, the hazard of living on the second floor. It was almost way too hot even in winter time. Marching over to the fridge, she was greeted with stale milk and expired yogurt. Dominic wasn't kidding when he said there was nothing to eat. She'd been working too much and shopping too little.

Kicking off her shoes, she dropped articles of clothing all the way to the bathroom. A quick shower and she might feel human enough to head to the grocery store. The water refreshed her and she took a few more minutes to wash her hair. It was amazing what a hot shower or bath could do for one's mood.

Turning the water off, she grabbed a towel and stepped out of the shower. Humidity had fogged up the mirror and with a whip of her hand she cleared it off. The face looking back at her had aged. She was only in her mid-twenties yet she felt much older.

Her tummy growled again as she began combing out her thick hair. If she didn't eat something soon, she'd pass out. There were several restaurants in town that did brunch, but right now she'd be lucky if she made it to the car and went to a drive-thru. Did any of them deliver? Hunger made her dizzy.

Opening the bathroom door, her towel brushed the comb she'd set on the sink and it fell to the floor. Stephanie turned and bent over to pick it up. Just doing that made the room spin a bit. Dang, she was starving. "Damn him." If he wouldn't have distracted her, she'd have eaten something for breakfast.

"Damn who?" a deep voice sounded from her living room.

Stephanie jumped and spun around. Dominic sat on her couch, sipping a cup of coffee. Just the smell of it caused her to take an involuntary step closer.

"What are you doing here? You scared the crap out of me. And how did you get in?" His eyes seemed to be focused on her legs. "Hey, up here." She motioned with her hands toward her face, but that just seemed to move his attention to her chest. "Answer me." Her heart raced and she was weak with hunger. There was only so much more she could take.

"You didn't have any food. I had bought you some but they sat in the truck so long, I threw them out and went back for more." He pointed to where a stack of to-go containers sat on the kitchen counter. The scent of bacon had penetrated the Styrofoam and she headed toward it like a hound dog on a scent. They were packed full of bacon, sausage links, scrambled eggs, French toast, and hash browns, and beside them sat a carton of milk and a bottle of orange juice. There was even a box of donuts. Dunkers! She'd died and gone to breakfast heaven.

The chocolate dunker was the first to touch her lips. It was her favorite. They came in three different flavors and were sold at the local gas station. Dunkers were a heavenly, old-style cake donut with a sugary glaze. She closed her eyes and enjoyed the chocolate flavor on her tongue. If Dominic wasn't here, she'd drink the milk straight from the jug. Her thoughts returned to the man in her living room and she spun around.

"Hey, how did you get in? I know I locked it."

He just sat there staring as if he hadn't heard a word. She took another bite of the dunker and a crumb fell on her chest. Stephanie looked to where it fell and the donut lodged in her throat. She'd been so caught up in the sight and smell of the treats that she hadn't realized she was naked. How had that happened?

Dominic got off the couch and picked up the towel that had fallen off halfway between the bathroom and the kitchen. Stephanie couldn't move except to breathe. Her chest rose and fell as she took deep breaths. Being nude and alone in her apartment with Dominic was something she'd only thought about late at night. This was the middle of the day. She turned around, dropped the donut back in the box it came in and sucked in her stomach. Her face was bright red yet she couldn't move.

He stepped closer and draped the towel over her

shoulders just like he had done with his coat the night before. She seized it and quickly covered herself. Shyness returned and her gaze settled on the floor. Stephanie swallowed as his hand turned her face back toward his. The man towered over her and his heated gaze focused on her lips. She'd never felt so small before.

"I can see why you went to these first. They taste sweet." Dominic brushed his finger over the bit of glaze that had settled on the side of her lip and sucked it into his mouth. "Just like you."

Chapter Ten

Dominic

It took everything he had to not throw Stephanie on the nearby bed and make love to her for the next twenty-four hours. He puffed out his cheeks and shook his head. She was a vision. It was a given that she had a great body as he'd seen her many times in shorts or workout wear when she jogged around the lake, but he never expected the impact seeing her naked would have on him. His dick stood at attention as soon as she'd stepped out of the bathroom draped only in that barely-there towel. When the white piece of cloth hit the floor, he thought his head would explode.

She looked like an angel. An angel who had firm breasts, full hips, and a slender waist. Her wet hair gave her a wild look that drew him even more. Taking a deep breath, he tried to calm his heart rate. Dominic had always prided himself on not being riled by anything. He'd seen it all, done it all, but Steph was a whole new ball game. There had only been one woman in his life, and when she was gone, everything ended. Dom didn't care if he ever had a woman again. Until now.

Dominic leaned back in the seat of his truck and glanced up toward her window. What a jerk he was. Licking the sugar from her lips like he was a love-sick puppy and then storming out. Her eyes had gotten big and she visibly shook. Fuck. He'd scared her and made an idiot of himself. To someone like Stephanie, the thought of being with him would probably be worse than death. Like a fool, he'd just left without a word. Everyone thought he was a savage, he should've just proven them right and taken her on the countertop like the animal he was. But then he'd never see her again, and that was something he couldn't live with. Not yet anyway.

The curtains in her window fluttered and he sat up straighter. Was she watching to see if he was gone? He pounded the steering wheel with his fist. There were no threats to her that they could find so he couldn't justify staying any longer. He'd continue to teach her how to defend herself but the chances of her wanting to see him again were doubtful. A bead of sweat rolled down his neck. It was hot for June. People always thought it was cold in Wisconsin but the heat and humidity made it almost unbearable at times.

Dominic started the truck and took one more glance at the window. She wasn't there. He loved solitude but right now he'd never felt more alone, and it didn't feel good at all. Scratching his beard, it took a few moments to decide what to do and where to go. Going home didn't seem like a good idea so he drove to Roman's. His boss was away spending time with his wife but Roman welcomed his men to use the workout room at his complex anytime.

It took him longer than usual now that the tourists were back in town. The guards waved him in as he passed through the gate of Roman's compound and Dom parked his truck by the gym. Swamp-like air struck him with full force as soon as he opened the door. It would be cooler in the front yard with the gentle breeze coming off the lake but enjoying the view was the last thing on his mind. He was here to purge a certain blonde beauty from his mind.

Chances were good that a storm was building. He paused as even that reminded him of Stephanie. The poor thing was terrified of bad weather but wouldn't share why. As much as he tried to deny it, he would be staking out her place later in case the skies took a turn for the worse. She'd probably think he was a stalker, and he was definitely starting to feel like one.

The cooler air of Roman's huge gym was a welcome relief. It was better than any fitness center. The equipment was first rate. There were always fresh towels, a great television, sound system, and top-notch showers. The place even had a sauna and hot tub. From the heavy breathing coming from around the corner, Dominic, unfortunately, wasn't alone. It was Jasper. He dropped his chin. *Son of a bitch.* That was all he needed, to spend more time with the guy. Dom stopped, cursed under his breath, and placed his hands on his hips.

"Hey, dude." The man was lifting weights.

"Thought you'd still be with that hot little blonde."

"What blonde?" Stephanie was the last thing he wanted to talk to Jasper about. Dominic tossed his keys on a nearby bench.

"Ha, you know." Jasper put the weights back in place and reached for a towel. His t-shirt was soaked, so the guy had obviously been at it for a while.

"No, I don't. What about you?" Dom pulled a pair of boxing gloves on and wandered over to the punching bag.

"Took that lady cop home." He winked. "Her name's Danny."

Dom snorted. "You slept with a cop? Are you nuts?"

"Hey, she's hot and crazy. Man, she did everything but handcuff my nuts and stick her baton up my ass." Jasper smiled and shook his head. "I think I'm in love."

Jasper was a known player and was making his way through most of the young women in town, maybe a few of the older ones as well. Working on his uppercut, Dom struck the bag with a vengeance. "You know that's asking for trouble." He gave it a sidekick.

"Some things are worth a little trouble." Jasper wiped his face with a towel and strolled over to Dom. "So did you fuck the chick or not?"

He didn't even think. He just acted. Dominic swung and hit Jasper square in the jaw. The guy staggered back and landed on his ass. Dom stood ready to attack again but Jasper just sat on the floor and laughed.

"I knew it. You're in love in with her."

"Shut the fuck up or I'll hit you again." His fists were still raised, eager to kick some ass, and this guy was his new favorite target.

"You know it's true." Jasper rested back on his hands, an open invitation to take another punch.

"Fuck you." Dominic rolled his eyes and gave the bag a series of hits that would put any living being in the hospital. He wasn't able to strike someone who wasn't going to fight back. Jasper was a killer just like the rest, but in their off time, the guys didn't battle. Roman's rules. Hopefully, he wouldn't catch hell for the punch to the man's face. "You don't know shit," Dom yelled between punches.

Jasper held the towel to his cheek and slowly rose to his feet. "You know. If you need some tips on the ladies, I'd be happy to help."

"Get lost. I'm not interested in her and I certainly don't need your help." Dom threw off the gloves and turned to the barbells next, lifting them one arm at a time.

"Yeah, keep telling yourself that."

"It's true." He matched his breaths to the lifts.

"You could've fooled me." Jasper winced as he sipped from his water bottle.

"Don't you ever shut up?" Dom had to fight the urge to toss the weights at the guy's head.

"What?" Jasper rolled his eyes. "Everyone loves to hear me talk."

"You're the only one who loves to hear you talk." Dominic mentally calculated the many ways he could kill Jasper and the various locations to bury his body. Unfortunately, Roman would be pissed, and killing a member of the family meant death for the killer as well.

"I think Miss Stephanie Barclay likes you. Not sure what she sees…different strokes for different folks, as they say. Maybe she likes to walk on the dark side." Jasper shrugged and wandered over to the window.

"She wouldn't be caught dead with a guy like me," Dominic muttered.

"Why not?" Jasper turned and walked back to his side.

"You know why." Dom sighed and put the weights down where they belonged. Maybe he needed to go for a run or something as this sure as hell wasn't working. Why the hell couldn't he just leave?

"No, I don't know why. And besides, you two are a couple of idiots. She was watching you all night and you were doing the same. You're both fucking stupid." Dominic turned fast and Jasper jumped back, putting his hands up. "I'm just trying to help."

"I don't need your help. Can't you just get the hell out of here?"

"Look, I know I joke around a lot but I can tell she means something to you. I got the feeling you think she's in some kind of danger. If you need backup, just let me know. You need someone to watch her when you can't, just let me know." His face was sincere.

"And why would you do that?" Dom narrowed his eyes and crossed his arms in front of his chest.

"Because we're brothers, man. Whether you like it or not. If you want a girl to love you, tell her your secrets." Jasper placed a hand on Dom's shoulder. "And she'll tell you hers. I'm out of here"

A lump formed in his throat. Not everyone was blood-related in Roman's crew but they would take a bullet for each other.

His family had perished years ago, before he'd been taken. When Roman Caponelli found him, he'd given him another chance at life. After what happened, Dominic had proclaimed himself a loner, but the older he got, the more he realized it wasn't enough anymore. Unfortunately, anyone who knew his secrets would never feel anything but disgust.

The phone in his bag buzzed.

"Hello?"

It was Roman's number but it was Madison who spoke. "Dom, I hate to ask, but I need a huge favor."

"Sure. What is it?" She didn't need to ask as he would never turn her down.

"I can't get a hold of Stephanie. I've left messages and she hasn't returned any. I'm a little worried."

"Maybe she just has the phone turned off."

"You're probably right, but I just wanted to make sure. I left a message early this morning but still nothing. She's supposed to pick up the gifts today with one of the guys and take them to Val and Ryan's house. I also wanted to talk to her about work tomorrow."

"I'm at the gym but I'll drive by on the way home and see where she's at."

"Thanks, Dom." Madison hung up.

If he hadn't just left her place he'd be worried, but it was a good chance her phone was in her car or turned off. Steph wasn't a phone person and barely used hers, if at all. She didn't have that many people to call.

Jasper was gone so he didn't have to deal with any more of his bullshit. After a quick shower, Dominic left the gym and drove to Steph's place. The last thing he wanted to do right now was talk to her. They both needed time apart, at least he did. Just being in the same room with her had him doubting everything he did or said. Maybe that dickhead Jasper was right, he did have it bad.

He drove slowly through town. The cars were now bumper to bumper. As soon as he could get on a side street, he took it. The town depended on tourists in the summer but it was a bitch to get around. Stephanie's street was quiet so he took a sweep through the back parking lot just to check. There were no bikes and her car wasn't there or out front.

He then checked Firenza. Nothing. They must have picked up the gifts and were dropping them off now. It was a long drive back the way he just came, as Val and Ryan were given the house next door to Roman as a wedding present from her father. It was a multi-million dollar gift, that was for sure. If he'd been thinking, he would have checked there before he left. The problem was when she was on his mind, he wasn't thinking.

With traffic, it took a half hour to get back to where he just was. The Donavans' driveway was empty. "Damn." He hit the number on his phone for the tech guys. "I need to find someone." Dom gave them the description of her vehicle. Using the many cameras they had around town, it still took a couple of minutes before they located her at a small coffee shop.

"Anything else you need, Dom?" the tech questioned.

"No." He paused. "Hey, wait. Can you get me a tracker for a car?"

"Sure. Where do you want it sent?" The tech guys would never give their location so he told them to leave it at the gatehouse and he'd pick it up tomorrow. If he wasn't a stalker before, he felt like one now. There would be no need for Madison to worry about her friend after tomorrow because he was putting a tracer on Stephanie's car.

"Also, I need you to do something else." He spied a cat prowling along the side of a house and it made him think of the smell back at her apartment.

"Sure. What do you need?"

"I want surveillance on a building." He gave them Stephanie's home address. "I think we might have someone cooking meth."

Chapter Eleven

Stephanie

This was turning out to be one of the longest days of her life. After Dominic left, she couldn't think straight. Rationalizing that it must be from hunger, Steph made a good dent in all the food he'd brought her. Feeling human again, she remembered she was in charge of making sure all the wedding gifts got to Ryan and Valentina's home. Surprisingly enough, it was Danny, one of Ryan's coworkers, and a couple of Roman's enforcers who met her at the club and helped carry the gifts out.

Roman had a ton of burly men to move things but it took two girls to get things organized. The guys may have known how to shake things down but they had no clue what fragile meant. A few even tossed the gifts back and forth before she could get them to stop. Their boss would be getting an earful when she saw him next. Actually, she tried to avoid the man as much as possible so chances were good she wouldn't be saying a thing.

Danny brought her pickup truck but it still took a couple of trips to get it all done. She liked Danny but the woman swore like a sailor and was a little too open about her personal life. Steph felt her face flush just thinking about some of the things she'd mentioned about her night with Jasper. At least it took her mind off of Dominic for a while.

Stephanie sipped her ice coffee. It was late in the day to be drinking caffeine but chances were good she wouldn't be sleeping much that night anyway. The weatherman had just issued a tornado watch for the evening. There was nothing she hated more than thunderstorms. It brought back memories best left in the past.

Her fingers clicked on the keys of her laptop. The coffee shop was only open until five and then she'd have to find somewhere else to go. There was no way she'd be spending a minute in the second story of her rickety apartment complex during a severe thunderstorm, not to mention a tornado. It was a good chance she'd be moving from place to place throughout the day until everything closed up for the night. After closing time, she might be sleeping in her car, afraid to go upstairs. Maybe if things got too bad, she could go to the town's storm shelter, she'd done that before.

So far, she was on a roll. The words flowed and there was a new hook to the storyline. A waitress set another iced coffee on the table and took her empty glass. She was dressed in a simple t-shirt with the store logo on the front. They must give free refills because she hadn't ordered one. Another hour passed and the place was now vacant. A coffee shop obviously had more of a morning rush than a late afternoon crowd.

"Is there anything else I can get you before we close?" The girl rested a hand on the empty chair at her table. In other words, they were kindly asking her to leave.

"No, just the check, please." Stephanie closed her laptop and started to gather her things.

"It's all taken care of, hon." The girl smiled.

"Huh?" The place was empty except for her and the staff. "By who?"

The girl just shrugged. "Not sure. I was just told you didn't owe a thing."

"Really? That's weird, but thank you." Maybe someone paid it forward. She heard about that happening on the news all the time. Stuffing everything into her bag, Steph told the staff goodbye and stepped out into the sultry air. The wind had picked up and a few leaves skidded across the parking lot. Stopping by her car, goosebumps rose on her arm. It was as if someone was watching her, but a scan of the surrounding area proved there was no one around. Probably just the effects of the storm freaking her out. Pretty soon, the hair on her head would be standing on end.

Stephanie drove to Pier 290. It was right on the lake where she'd gone for yoga on the beach a few times. The restaurant had a great vibe and she loved that it opened right out to the water. Taking a seat, Stephanie jumped at a flash of lightning. Maybe it wasn't such a good idea to be sitting outside. The waitress assured her that as long as it didn't start raining she'd be fine. The storm was still a long way off according to the television in the bar. Despite just having several glasses of ice coffee, Stephanie ordered fish tacos and a glass of wine. Their tacos were the best in town.

She'd left her computer in the car and brought in a book to read. It felt good just to sit and stare at the clear water and the few passing boats that were not afraid of the impending storm. The lake was famous for the wooden boats that all the lake homers seemed to have. Most were in the $200,000 and up range. Roman had one, but then what didn't he have. Hours passed as she sipped her wine and savored the great food. The evening sky had darkened and it was closing time. As much as she dreaded it, it was time to go home.

Stephanie waved down her server. "Can I just get the bill?"

"It's been taken care of, and a very generous tip also." She smiled.

"What?" An unsettling sense of déjà vu surrounded her. "By who?"

"Not sure. The bartender just said it was taken care of." The young lady gathered Stephanie's empty plate and utensils. "Have a good night."

"Uh, thanks." Stephanie hesitated. The thought that someone was following her around and paying her bills was starting to freak her out. At least they were a generous lurker.

It was a Sunday night, so the place closed earlier than other nights, but, fortunately, it wasn't too dark out yet despite the gloomy sky. Still, she held her purse and book close to her body like a shield.

Killing more time, Stephanie studied some of the

displays on the hallway walls as she left. There was even a vintage Playboy bunny costume from when there used to be one of Hugh Hefner's clubs on the lake. The lights above were boat propellers, which were a fun accent. Not able to stall any longer, she stepped outside. Luckily, there was no boogeyman ready to jump her. The storm seemed to have passed further to the south but it was still warm. Light shown through the windows of a nearby boat builder and customers could be seen checking out the vessels. They must have had a late-night appointment. For what they paid for the boats, it was a good bet they'd open at midnight if someone suddenly had the urge to purchase one.

Her car sat under the light pole and she checked the backseat before unlocking it and getting in. It never hurt to be careful.

She couldn't put it off any longer. It was time to go home. When she was just about to pull out of the parking lot, something caught her eye. A familiar truck flicked on its lights and tailed her out. Her heart stopped and she had to take several deep breaths to calm down.

It wasn't some Good Samaritan who had paid for her drinks and meals. It was Dominic in the shadows. He'd been totally invisible until now. Did he suspect she'd be on guard and he didn't want to scare her any more than she was? He confused the hell out of her. Was she still in danger when he said not to worry? Had he become her protector for some weird, kinky reason? She really knew nothing about the man. At least he'd left of his own free will when she was at her most vulnerable earlier in the day. Dom was a lot taller and stronger than her. If he really wanted to, he could've raped, killed, and buried her, and no one would have known what happened to her. That was his job, making people disappear, but she'd never heard of him doing any harm to women. Roman wouldn't allow any of his men to do that. Apparently, Dom didn't dance or date either, but he'd kind of danced with her.

The man kept his distance as he shadowed her on the main road back to town. It was both frightening and reassuring at the same time. The radio confirmed that the threat of a storm had bypassed Genoa but would probably stir back up for tomorrow. It was typical weather for this time of year. Hot and steamy followed by a cold front that often plowed through anything in its path. Downtown Genoa was quiet for a Sunday evening in June.

When she turned down her street and he followed, a knot formed in her gut. She couldn't deal with him anymore today, or anyone for that matter. It'd been a long weekend and she had to get up for work early tomorrow. Madison and Valentina may be off enjoying time with their men but she had no one. Dom's headlights flickered in her rearview mirror as his truck drove over a speed bump. She had no one but the enigma that was Dominic Scarlatti.

She parked her car in the front, grabbed her things, and locked the car. Hurrying to the front door, she ran in and closed it quickly behind her. Watching out the peephole, she noticed his truck slow but it kept going. Stephanie let out a deep breath and leaned her back against the door. She should have felt relieved, but, surprisingly, all she felt was disappointment. The place was empty and quiet except for the noise of a television coming from behind one door. Someone was watching a talk show, laughter cutting in every now and then. Her footsteps creaked on the old stairs. It wouldn't surprise her if someone's foot went right through them someday. The whole place should be condemned, but then where would she live?

The usual rotten egg smell kicked in by the time she reached the top. She really needed to contact the super about that, but he would just say, "Yeah, I'll add that to my list." Stephanie opened the door to her apartment. The humid air kicked up the smell of bacon from the leftover takeout containers. She quickly turned on the fans. The place didn't have air conditioning but at least the windows still opened and weren't painted shut.

Her bags found their home on the couch and she settled in next to them. The whole world seemed out of sync. Why did today seem lonelier than any other day? Why did Dom just walk out the door this morning when she stood there naked? At first, she'd been thankful, but now she questioned her appeal to members of the opposite sex. Did men not find her attractive, or was it just the "I don't want to get involved" vibe she gave off?

Not too long ago, Dominic had kissed her. He'd grabbed her and pressed his lips to hers. Her fingers automatically rose to touch her mouth. Saying who was more shocked would be a toss-up. It was a panty dropping kiss if she'd ever had one. As much as she tried to deny it, he intrigued her like no one ever had. Her knees went weak whenever he was around and even sometimes when she pictured him in her mind. So far, he'd kept his distance. That fact should have relieved her, but for some reason, it didn't.

Things had not been easy since leaving California, leaving everything and everyone she'd known her entire life.

The first couple of years were the worst. Every shadow made her jump. Every stranger was a threat. Every man who looked at her made her flesh crawl—every man but Dominic. She twirled a strand of hair around her finger. In her former life, she wouldn't have given the guy a passing glance. Not just because of his profession, but because of his appearance. Before, she only ever went out with the clean-cut guys approved by her father. Ones who never had a hair out of place, a tattoo, or who drove a car worth less than half a million. Boy, had things changed.

Men she thought were above reproach turned out to be lower than dirt and not trustworthy at all. Especially the one she thought she'd spend her life with. Even when her dad knew what the man was capable of he still insisted she go through with the nuptials. It was about honor, he'd said. The family would lose respect if she didn't. Her fiancé was just working his way to the top by taking risks. Risks like being in the sex trade and human trafficking business. Her father didn't believe how dirty the guy was and wanted to believe the best of the young man. She hoped and prayed that he knew the truth now.

Chapter Twelve

Dominic

He was running on fumes but managed to get a few hours' sleep. When the fuck was Arlo getting back? Dominic half closed his eyes as he watched the scared shitless prospect tied up to a chair. His patch proclaimed him as Square. What kind of a name was that? They were in an old shed out in the country. Who owned it, he wasn't sure and didn't care. It was above his pay grade. A bead of sweat ran down his back. The heat index had to be in the upper nineties.

Dominic stood by the open door. Jasper had just finished tying the guy up and was walking toward him and the welcome breeze from outside. Even he had shed the designer threads today but still wore a dress shirt and light-colored pants.

"Hotter than a bitch today." Jasper pulled at his shirt to keep it from sticking to his chest.

Dominic glanced at his feet. "What the hell are you wearing? Pajamas?"

Jasper sighed and rolled his eyes. "Linen pants. It wouldn't hurt your image to give up the 'serial killer who lives in the woods' look."

"Is it easy to get blood out of that shit?" Dom kept his eyes on the prospect. Jasper was new and he didn't always trust that his knot tying skills, as well as other things, were up to snuff.

"Well, no. I have to dry clean them." Jasper crossed his arms in front of his chest and leaned against the wall.

"Then I'll stick with what I've got." Dominic glanced at his watch. He had better things to do than listen to fashion tips from a nimrod. "What time is Roman getting here?"

"Soon. Arlo got back today so he's just waiting for him to pick him up."

Genoa was safe enough but one never knew. It wouldn't be good for the boss to be on his own. Roman was a fierce fighter, but if he were ambushed, he'd be a goner. Finally, a black SUV came flying down the road. The tires ground to a stop on the crushed rock and a cloud of dust stirred up.

Roman's right-hand man, Arlo, stepped out first. Dark sunglasses hid his eyes but he nodded in their direction. The man was huge and they often joked that he should play for the Green Bay Packers. His dress shoes crunched on the gravel as he strolled over to open the door for their boss. Even an idiot could pick out Roman from a lineup as the man in charge. He radiated control, confidence, and danger. It always amazed him how Madison could get the guy to do almost anything, but she was the only one.

Today, he'd shed his suit coat but still had on his usual dark dress pants and crisp white shirt. His red tie blew in the breeze. Roman wore a shoulder holster with two guns firmly in place under each arm. When he walked into the building, he handed his designer shades to Jasper and turned his back to the prisoner.

"Did he say anything yet?" His jaw was set and he rested his hands on his hips. The man didn't mess around.

"No, just bullshit about why did we take him, why is he here," Jasper answered. "Why is he here?" They hadn't asked when they got the order, just did what was told.

"Someone's dealing drugs in town. I don't want that shit around the schools. They can deal out of town, and I don't care what the rich bastards around the lake do in their homes, but we have a deal with the club and I want to see what's going on." Roman waited as both men nodded. Arlo was still outside as the lookout.

From what Dominic understood, the Tribe of Mayhem Club could run drugs without competition anywhere in the county, just not in the city limits. It was a virtual safe zone. In an unspoken agreement with local law enforcement, the Caponelli family kept crime out, and in return, the cops kept their nose out of the family's businesses.

Jasper and Dom stayed where they were as Roman walked to the center of the room. It was well known what had happened to the man who kidnapped Madison when they'd first met. The guy had been tied to a chair just like this poor kid. With one kick, his boss had sent the man backward. Everyone in the room heard the crack of his skull on the concrete and then the fire of his gun as Roman shot him between the eyes.

The prospect tried to scoot his chair back but it didn't budge. He probably shit his pants when Roman calmly placed his foot on the edge between the kid's knees. Even with the dust, Dominic could see the shine on his fancy shoes. Jasper once told him they were Ferragamo or something like that and cost over a thousand dollars. If he had a grand, he'd probably buy something for Stephanie, not buy footwear. She needed a better car and a decent place to live, but chances were good the woman would never accept charity. He'd have to do it anonymously like he'd paid her tabs last night.

"What do you want from me?" the prospect squealed.

"Simple." Roman put his foot on the ground. "Just some info and you can be on your way."

"I don't know anything. I'm just a prospect."

"You have eyes. What have you seen?"

"I don't know what you mean," the kid said, shaking his head.

"Let me narrow it down for you. Who in your club is dealing in town?"

Square frowned. "In town? That's rule number one. Don't let anything go down in Genoa or the Caponellis will put you in the lake feet first. That's the one thing that will get you thrown out of the club, no questions asked. The president is adamant about that. If something is going down in town, it isn't one of the Mayhem. I don't know much but I do know that."

Roman took a step back but gave the kid a hard stare. Square glanced back and forth between the boss and the two of them still standing by the door.

"So who is dealing in town?" His boss spoke low but Dom could still hear what he said.

"Talk is some rednecks out in the country. They had a meth lab but it got torched."

Jasper elbowed him in the ribs. "Wonder who did that?"

Dominic wasn't much of a drinker, but if he had to be around this guy any longer, he'd need a shot of something.

"Obviously, they didn't get the message. Do they have any other locations that you know of?" Roman wouldn't leave until he learned everything he came to hear, and Square seemed more than willing to talk.

"No, just heard rumors that there's a lab in town. Not sure where."

"You're sure?" Roman stepped closed and placed his foot back between the boy's knees again.

"I swear on my life." The guy nodded vigorously. "If my hands were free, I'd cross my heart."

"Anything else you care to share?" Roman grabbed the kid by the back of his neck.

"No, sir."

Roman stared at him for a few moments before straightening and walking their direction. He sent a text message and then slipped his phone in his pants pocket. They all knew the kid told the truth, but what did they do with him now?

"I questioned Forge about these activities earlier. He said the same thing but I wanted to see what someone lower in the ranks knew." Forge was the president of the Tribe of Mayhem, and another biker with a fucked up name. Roman nodded to where Square sat. "I just texted him that we found his prospect broke down out here. Untie him and poke a hole in his tire."

"Will they know we questioned him?" Jasper asked, and handed back the gold sunglasses he'd been left in charge of.

"Of course, but rough him up a bit so it looks like he put up a fight. I don't think they're the ones crossing us but send the message anyway." He patted Jasper on the shoulder and glanced Dominic's way. "Dom, a word outside."

They left Jasper to do the dirty work. Square would have a few cuts and bruises but he'd live to brag about it later at the bar. He might even pick up a few chicks with the new black and blue marks.

"Stephanie say any more about her friend's son? Or of anything else like that going on in town?"

Dom shook his head and lifted his hair over his shoulder. Long hair wasn't the brightest idea during the summer but he wasn't cutting it after all these years. "No."

"I've noticed you've been spending some time with her. Anything going on? Anything related to what happened in April that I need to know about?"

Dominic rested his backside against the SUV. The hot metal caused him to sweat even more, or maybe it was just the question. He brushed his hair away from his face again and groaned.

"You know how she is. Can't get any answers. There's something off, just don't know what it is."

"I don't trust her. Get me a fingerprint and we'll run it. Otherwise, she's gone," Roman demanded.

"What?" Dom stood up. A cloud crossed the sunny sky and shaded his face.

"I don't like that my wife's best friend has so many secrets. The whole deal with her car having fake plates, no driver's license, and then I find out that Maddy's been paying her cash all this time."

"Huh?" That he didn't know.

"I just found that out today. She's never claimed Steph on the payroll. It's been all under the table. The tax implications alone are a mess. I told Madison she has to do the paperwork on her by tomorrow or she's out of here. Friends or not. Tax evasion brought Capone down, I'll be damned if some little no-named blonde will be the end of me."

"So what do you want me to do about it?" His heart dropped to his knees. Roman could end her life with a flick of his fingers. The thought of having to dispose of her beautiful body made him physically sick and his vision blurred. Dominic rubbed the back of his hand against his beard.

"Find out who Stephanie really is. If she doesn't talk, get me the fingerprint. Soon." Roman moved toward the car and placed his hand on the door handle. "This matter's been going on for far too long."

"Yeah," he spat, and Roman turned around. He'd never been disrespectful, but as much as he tried to deny it, he wanted to protect Stephanie, wanted her for himself, secrets and all.

"What did you say?" Roman folded his arms in front of his chest and Arlo joined his side.

"I said yes. I will do what you ask."

Roman told Arlo to get in the car. After the driver's side door closed, Roman whispered in Dom's ear. "I know you think because of what happened in the past women are off limits, but you are one of the best men I know. Don't let the wrong one bring you down."

Dom dropped his chin to his chest. Never did he think he'd be having this conversation. "She isn't wrong. She's hiding from someone, I just don't know who."

"Then find out before it's too late." His boss patted his shoulder and sighed. "And if she's clean, make her yours."

"I don't—"

"Cut the crap, everyone can see you two have the hots for each other. Check her out before it's too late. Understand?"

"Yes."

Dominic stepped back as Roman got in the car. The tires spun on the gravel as they took off down the road. A strong wind blew the dust they'd stirred up and he turned his back.

He'd been watching from the sidelines for too long. The thought of losing something he never had kicked him in the gut. As soon as he got to town, Steph was coming with him whether she wanted to or not. She wouldn't respond to threats so he would try another way.

Dominic trusted Roman with his life. If he

thought he should take a chance, he would. Stephanie Barclay was the one he wanted, but if he pushed, she would flee like a frightened deer. What he had to do was get her to trust him, and that might just prove to be one of the hardest things he's ever had to do. If Roman called for her death, there was no way Dominic would ever let that happen, and Genoa would see a shit storm hit the town with more force than a tornado.

Chapter Thirteen

Jasper ended up knocking Square out with a lucky blow. By the time he woke up, the Tribe had roared in to get him. They weren't happy to find their prospect beat up and two of Roman's crew there when they arrived.

It was touch and go for a bit as to whether or not they would be getting out of there alive. Square woke up and informed Forge that Jasper and Dom had stopped to help when they saw his bike stalled. After that, he and Jasper had exchanged blows over some girl, but then he had slipped on some loose dirt and knocked himself out. Forge knew what the deal was as he'd just heard from Roman, but he never let on.

Dominic and Jasper probably owed the prospect their lives as it was about twenty to two, and to top it off they were packing some of the guns that they'd purchased from Roman. Dom had helped unload the last shipment of firearms and ammo.

Things with the Tribe settled, it took longer than Dominic expected to make it back to town He had never been so happy to see Genoa. Even with all the tourists starting to arrive it was a welcome sight. A better sight would be coming home to Stephanie writing one of her stories on his front porch, but that was just a dream.

"Want to get some lunch?" Jasper mumbled while swiping through his phone.

"It's four in the afternoon."

"Got anything better to do?" He glanced at a long-legged brunette waiting for the walk light to change. "I see something I'd like to do."

"Fuck, is that all you ever think about?" Dominic shook his head. The man had a one-track mind.

"Not always, but most of the time. So what do you say? I'm starving."

"Okay." Dom finally caved. Stephanie would still be at work anyway.

"Really?" Jasper raised an eyebrow.

"Yeah, where to?" He kept driving but Jasper said nothing. "Where?" Dominic glanced his way.

"Sorry, I'm in shock." Jasper laughed.

"Don't have anywhere to be, might as well eat." It was hard being around other people except for the Caponellis, but he was trying to make an effort. One would think spending what amounted to years in near solitary confinement would make him never want to be alone again, but he'd found contentment in being by himself. That was until Stephanie spent one night at his house a couple of months ago. Since then, the place only seemed lonely.

"So, you want to hit the clubs later?" Jasper asked.

"Don't press your luck."

"Buzzkill." The man practically pouted. Didn't he have any friends?

"Where do you want to eat?" Dom asked again.

Jasper mentioned one of the trendy lakeside bars but Dom shot it down as being too busy. Crowds still put him on edge and in "fight to kill" mode. They finally settled on a place a little further down the lakeshore.

The wind caused whitecaps out on the water but they still ate on the patio. Jasper ordered a burger and fries while Dominic had deep fried cheese curds and a fire oven pizza. The cheese melted in his mouth as he bit into the salty appetizer. This place made great ones as they didn't use a lot of batter. Being from Italy, he'd loved cheese as a kid. After he was taken, food was limited to protein and bland bread. Ever since then, he had never taken it for granted.

When Roman brought him to Chicago, it was hard to keep the tears from falling the first time he had a good meal. The Caponellis had welcomed him into their home but realized he needed space. For years, Dominic had basically lived in a cage, only allowed out for training and battles. Roman found him a small apartment in one of the buildings they owned. The emptiness of it reminded him of Stephanie's flat. It was just a place to rest his head until he found a real home.

The Windy City was all right, but when Roman moved to Genoa it was a blessing in disguise. The first time Dom saw it he was in heaven. The water reminded him of his childhood with his family and it always calmed him when he was on edge. He hadn't had a nightmare since he settled into his cabin by the lake. It was a good bet that Stephanie had bad dreams.

"Hey! Did you hear what I said?" Jasper snapped his fingers. The guy had just hit a high level of annoying and it was time to part ways.

"I said I'd eat with you, that didn't mean I had to listen to you talk." He took a bite of the pizza. It had olives, artichokes, capers, and sun dried tomatoes. It was as close to Italy as he'd ever be again. There was nothing and no one to go back for. His parents died when he was in his last year of school. But it was what happened to his girlfriend that cut him the most. The pizza lodged in his throat just thinking about it.

Dominic fought his way out of the dark fog that wandered into his thoughts. The past was the past. He had to stop living in it before the memories killed him. For the rest of his life, he'd be messed up in the head from what happened but there was no way he'd let the bastards who took him win. Some way, somehow, he would take his life back and hopefully end theirs.

The waitress returned. Jasper winked, asked for the check, and her number. They drove in silence until he dropped Jasper off at his place. Dominic sat there for a few minutes. As much as he wanted to see Stephanie, no, yearned to see Stephanie, something was holding him back. He didn't feel good enough for her. She was a nice girl, not one who would be content in a mafia family. She'd made her dislike of Roman well known to his wife many times. Only around Roman, Madison, and

Valentina did he feel human. They knew who he really was and still accepted him as family. Would Stephanie ever feel the same?

He glanced at his watch. The bridal store was closed but this was the night she volunteered. Putting his truck in gear, he headed to the Genoa Arts Center. The parking lot was crowded with cars. He backed into a parking spot so the driver's side was in the shade and rolled down the window. There was no way he'd go inside. Somewhere around three, he'd reached his limit for human contact for the day. Yet he wanted to see her.

Stephanie's car was parked in the far corner of the lot. At least the place closed at eight, so it would still be light out when she was done. She'd be getting a talking to about unsafe parking but chances were good she knew what she was doing. He glanced at his watch and cursed. It was only six. What the hell was he going to do for two hours? He pulled out his cell phone and started to read a book. It was one of the few normal things that he really enjoyed. A cool breeze off the lake helped keep the heat at a bearable level. Dominic became lost in the words for an hour.

Near closing time, the place had emptied out. Getting out of the truck, he headed into the center. His alone time with the book had put him in a better mood, but what was he going to say to Stephanie to get her to confess her life story? He wouldn't get any answers sitting outside. As he entered the place the cool air was a welcome relief. The emptiness of it felt even better.

"Hello. Can I help..." The bright smile she had

dropped when Stephanie saw it was him.

"What? Not happy to see me?" His boots sounded on the wood floor as he approached.

She folded her arms across her chest and his eyes briefly dropped to her boobs. "Well, bad things seem to happen when you're around."

"If I remember correctly, bad things seem to happen to you when I'm not around. I just happen to be the one who gets to clean up the mess."

"Well, that's what you do best. Isn't it? Clean?" Stephanie lifted her eyebrow.

"What's gotten into you?" He stopped in front of her and put his hands on her shoulders.

"Nothing." She slid out of his reach and behind the counter.

"Nothing?" Dominic placed his hands on the glass top.

Steph took a deep breath and twirled a piece of her hair. Yes, something was up. "I've been thinking."

"Ha, there's your problem right there." The words were out of his mouth before he could stop them.

"What did you say?" Her green eyes were wide and her cheeks flushed.

"What I meant to say was maybe if you shared some of your problems, you wouldn't have to be worrying about them so much." Whatever was wrong, he needed to find out what it was and soon.

"Why do you want to help me?" Her head was tilted down but her eyes looked up.

"Why shouldn't I?"

"Stop answering a question with a question." Her

tan skin reflected the light from the side window. The woman took his breath away like no other but he knew when to give in and just raise his hands in surrender. "Look, I appreciate what you've done for me, what you did for me, but I'm starting to feel like you're stalking me."

"I'm protecting you." Whether she wanted it or not. Did that make him a stalker? Maybe. He did order that tracker for her car.

"I don't need protection."

Roman's words floated through his mind. "I disagree," he said softly.

"Do you know something that I don't?" She fidgeted with her hair again.

"Maybe." If he told her that Roman only gave him days to find out about her past, she'd be gone in a flash.

"Ugh. You're driving me crazy." She placed her hands on both sides of her skull.

"Go out with me tonight," he blurted out. *What the hell?* He'd spent too much time out in the heat, he was talking crazy. When was the last time he asked someone out? He hooked up with chicks when the urge hit—the Caponellis had a club back in the city for just that very reason—but while it satisfied the itch, it did nothing to quell the yearning for love and acceptance. This was insane. He was insane, but it might be the only way to make her stay and gain her trust. Become the man she wrote about in her books.

"What?" Stephanie dropped the strand of hair from her finger.

He leaned across the counter and spoke quietly.

"Now who's answering a question with a question?"

She rolled her eyes, folded her arms across her chest again, and leaned on the back counter.

"And another thing." He made sure to stare into her eyes. Telling her that every time she put her arms under her breasts and pushed them up just made him want her more would have her fleeing to Michigan. She was stunning standing there looking fierce, feisty, and very flustered.

She was wearing a frilly yellow tank top and slender white capris. On her feet were high-heeled sandals and there was pretty pink polish on her toenails. He'd been spending too much time with Jasper if he was starting to notice things like that.

"Go on." Stephanie rocked from her toes to her heels and back.

Luckily, he was saved by the bell. Literally, the bell over the front door rang and Stephanie rushed to greet the visitor. "You have to go now," she called over her shoulder to Dom.

"I'll be waiting outside." He left without waiting for a rebuke.

Ten minutes later, he almost missed the click of Stephanie's sandals as she hurried to her car.

He tossed the phone on the seat of his truck and rushed after her.

"Hey!" His voice rang across the now empty lot but she didn't stop. Before she could reach her car, he grabbed her by the arm. "I said stop."

She tilted her head to the side. "Why are you following me? I appreciate all you've done for me and your offer to teach me self-defense but...but why are you here?" Her eyes seemed to search his. Their color was a deep bluish green.

"Because ever since I kissed you, I can't get you out of my mind. I want to take you out." There, he'd said it. Bared his soul like never before and she just stood there in shock. He wasn't like Jasper, not a Casanova. He hadn't been on a date in years. Time stood still and yet she remained mute. Well, screw her. Roman could off her for all he cared. So what if he spent the rest of his life alone. At least he didn't have to deal with the hurt and rejection of unanswered affection or of a loved one taken from him. Dejected, he turned and headed back to his truck.

"Wait," Stephanie called, and he halted. Her footsteps came closer and he felt the touch of her fingers on his arm. "Okay."

"Okay, what?"

She spoke softly. "Okay, I'll go."

Chapter Fourteen

Stephanie

Stephanie always knew the day would come when Dominic would follow up on his demands. It never dawned on her that he'd wish to take her on a date, that she'd been on his mind ever since that kiss. The kiss that had set her on fire yet frightened her to no end. It was easy to say it was just the emotion from almost being killed and being grateful to be alive, but it had been so much more.

Was it that they were both isolated in their own nightmares and craved any kind of affection they could get? No, the man had that bad boy image that drove women crazy. She also had turned down her share of offers for dates. They weren't guys that she knew very well but occasionally a tourist at the art center would ask her to show him around the town or a friend of the bride might want a date for the wedding. None of them caused her heart to race like Dom did.

They'd gone to the Pier, the same place by the

beach that he'd followed her to the day before. She knew nothing of this man sitting across the table from her. Did he even know himself? The last thing she needed was a lurker or to be the obsession of an unhinged beast that disposed of bodies for a living. The eccentric craftsman she could handle. The recluse with a shed full of knives, no way.

Her father had thought Maksim was a perfect angel, but he was worse than the devil. Appearances were deceiving. She herself was using a false name. So far, Dominic had been nothing but respectful and polite. Madison and Valentina wouldn't be trying to push them together if they thought he would be a danger to her.

"You like it here?" They were sitting out on the beach on lounge chairs, a small table between them. The sun hadn't set yet but the sky was already colorful and bright.

"I like being by the water." It relaxed her.

"What can I get you?" A waitress arrived with a pad in hand. Her nametag said "Brittany" in gold lettering.

Dominic turned in his chair toward Stephanie, indicating that she order first. "Uh, I guess I'll have a glass of white wine."

"And for you, sir?"

"I'll have a glass of red. Oh, and bring us an order of artichoke dip, island shrimp, and some cheese curds."

"Got it." She jotted it down on the pad with a pencil and left.

"Wow, that's not what I expected." Stephanie smirked.

"What, did you think I only drink blood and ate small children?" His eyes were intense in the dim light and he reminded her of a pirate with his long hair gently blowing in the evening breeze. The man was always hard to read but tonight it was as if a wide range of emotions were battling it out for dominance in his head.

"Well, no, but..." They were both silent for several moments. An awkward quiet settled over the table until Brittany returned with their drinks. They both said thanks and each took a sip, Dominic downing half of his.

"Where are you from?" Dominic placed his wine glass on the table while his fingers lingered on the stem. His hand so near hers that she could feel the electricity between them.

Suspicion kicked in. So this was why he was being so nice and asked her out.

"Where are you from?" Two could play at this game.

Steph almost fell off the chair when he answered, "Italy."

"I remember someone mentioning that. You don't have much of an accent though." It just dawned on her that he had spoken to Valentina in Italian once. How could she have forgotten? That deep voice speaking a foreign language would make any woman jump into his bed.

"I didn't speak English until I was in my teens but from then on it was all I spoke. Sometimes when I drink too much or get worked up it comes back." He winked and it made her knees weak. This was not the Dominic she knew but definitely one she could get used to.

"How many languages do you speak?" She took her last sip of wine. Stephanie stared at her empty flute. How did that happen so fast?

"A few." He motioned for Brittany to get them another round of drinks.

"So where are you from?" His dark eyes pulled her in as he asked again.

What harm could there be in answering? "California."

"How did you end up here?" Dom placed his hand on hers.

"You know I can't tell you." She slipped from his grasp.

"You can tell me anything and I won't tell a soul."

"No, I can't." As much as she tried to dislike the man there was something about him that drew her in. It was a game he was playing for information. She was the mouse to his cat. His confession could be fake, just like all the sweet things Maksim told her. Dominic worked for Roman, and his men had to do everything he ordered them to do.

Brittany set their appetizers and the second round of drinks on the table.

"I think you can tell me." He wasn't letting the subject drop as he reached for a curd and popped it in his mouth. "I'm willing to take the risk." Again, the charming smile crossed his lips, encouraging her to loosen hers.

Was he worth the risk? Dominic appeared to be a man who could survive anything, but surviving day to day had worn on her. All the years of keeping everything inside and letting nothing out was taking its toll. He'd taken care of Handlebar for her, it would be best if he knew why, but there were still a few things that could never be told.

"Let's just say I know some information that would put a lot of people in prison, yet if I told, it would put others at risk." There, she'd said it. Stephanie avoided his gaze as she dipped a chip in the dip.

"What if we could help you and any others?"

"You can't guarantee that." The dip was heavenly but right now nothing sat well with her stomach.

"We can't guarantee anything when we have no clue what the hell is going on. Please, Stephanie, let us help you." His voice had a tinge of an accent this time and she turned to face him. At one time, Stephanie thought she was a good judge of character, but that was a long time ago. Now, she had no clue who to trust.

"Thanks. I'll keep it in mind. Did you find anything out about who might be selling drugs in town?" Hopefully, her change in subject would mean there would be no more talk about her past.

"We discussed it with the Mayhem Tribe. They haven't violated any of our agreements. Together we had found a rogue meth lab but that was taken care of. Let us know if you hear of any more drugs floating around town. Roman doesn't give a shit about what the rich rock stars do in their own homes around the lake but he has a no selling to kids or around schools policy in town that is not to be violated by anyone."

"How very noble of him." It was an attempt to be a smartass, but to tell the truth, she agreed with it. Who cared what people did in their own homes, but kids needed to be protected. If Roman could help with that, so be it.

"He's very noble," Dominic added, and Steph rolled her eyes. "He saved me."

"You? Why would you ever need to be rescued?"

"He found me in a very bad place, covered in blood." The sun had set and his face was hard to read in the dim light. "Roman brought me back from the dead."

"Were you in an accident?" She hesitated to ask. For him to share something of his past was too much to resist.

"No." He wasn't taking the bait.

"Then what happened? You can't lay something out like that and then not tell the rest of the story."

"You just did." Dominic picked up a piece of shrimp and held it out for her to take a bite. Now he was feeding her? The whole thing felt like a setup. She took a bite anyway.

"That's different. Like I said, if I tell, people could die. Innocent people."

"Who's to say that won't happen if I tell you my story?"

It was true. She didn't know what had happened in his life. Had he been the victim of a crime? Was he as wary of others as she was? Stephanie focused on the water again. All she'd accomplished tonight was to fall further under his spell. She needed to find the skeletons in his closet just as much as he did hers.

"When can I have more classes?"

"Are you still concerned about the biker?" Dominic folded his arms over his chest.

"I don't know, but I'm tired of running. I don't have anywhere else to go." He started to speak but she interrupted. "It's been a long time since I had anyone to trust but you did save me and you never told anyone. If these people do show up someday, at least I know I can go to Roman as a last resort."

Dominic placed one hand on the table. "Roman isn't going to wait around for long. He's suspicious of those with secrets. You have to come clean soon." It was as if he was going to say more but his eyes said it all. He couldn't help her if she didn't want any, and he had no power over Roman.

"I'll keep it in mind. So would tomorrow night around six work for you?

He exhaled. "Yeah, meet me at the gym in town. I'll bring Jasper. You can beat the shit out of him."

She laughed. "I'd like that."

A smile threatened his lips. "Yeah, me too. Should we go?"

Dominic paid and they walked out the door. "You all right to drive?"

"Of course. I only had two glasses of wine and live a mile away." It'd been on the tip of her tongue to admit she was Russian and could hold her liquor but that would just open her up to more questions.

"I'll follow you home." With a hand to her lower back, Dominic guided her toward the exit. She never figured him for a touchy-feely kind of guy but it seemed natural when he reached out to her. Often,

Stephanie had heard Madison and Valentina whisper about him as having "issues" or "difficulties," yet they often encouraged her to get together with the man. It never made sense but maybe they were just two broken pieces that might mend together.

Stuffy air greeted them in the parking lot. The breeze from the lake was cut off by the building. Again, Dominic was the perfect gentleman and opened her car door. His attentive behavior, or maybe it was the wine, had her brain a jumbled mess. She started the engine and drove off just as his headlights turned on.

Covering a yawn with her hand, she turned down her street. When there was no traffic it never took more than ten minutes to get most places in town. Stephanie pulled up to the curb and parked under the street light. Crossing the street, she turned at the door to wave but the guy pulled in right behind her car.

This couldn't happen. If Dom thought she was going to invite him in, he had another think coming. They had a complicated relationship as it was. No, make that complicated acquaintance. She marched down the sidewalk to stop him from getting out of the truck.

Dominic's long legs had him meeting her before she could even make it to his door.

"Look…" she started.

"I want to kiss you again. Just say no if you don't want me to." His hand framed her face and he brushed his thumb across her lips.

What was she going to tell him? His eyes

seemed to erase all cells from her brain. She had a thought somewhere about not wanting to get involved but that was MIA also. How could someone want another but also be afraid to give in for fear of losing themselves?

As soon as his mouth touched hers, none of it mattered. Those large hands of his moved to her waist and pulled her closer. Her heart raced. Stephanie did what she'd been dying to do for so long. She threaded her fingers through his long hair. It was soft and thick. With a sigh, he slipped his tongue in. The man tasted of red wine and garlic with the shrimp. They were now her two favorite things in the world. Dominic tasted like heaven.

Never in a million years did she ever think she'd be standing in the middle of the street crushed to the chest of a man she knew nothing about. A man she was pretty sure she didn't want to know everything about. When he ended the kiss, he smiled. A stunning smile, and something so rare, it took her breath away. It made him appear younger and without a care.

Her life had been full of ups and downs, some good and some bad, but right now the highlight of it all was this moment. This moment in time that Dominic Scarlatti kissed her under a street light in the middle of the road.

Chapter Fifteen

Dominic

It was a fucked-up day. He was driving to one of the family's funeral homes. It had some Norwegian name like Olson, Gunderson, or Anderson, but it was owned by the Caponellis. Burying bodies in a field or at the bottom of the lake went out with landlines and VCRs. Now he usually just took them to the crematorium. There were no holes to dig and, most importantly, no DNA left behind. As long as he didn't get stopped for any traffic violations, everything would be good.

Today, he was driving the cleaner van, and, thankfully, that came with air conditioning. The sun beat through the windows but the body in the back hadn't started to smell yet.

It wasn't a mob hit. The unfortunate stiff in the back was courtesy of the Mayhem Tribe. Roman had lent his services to Forge in exchange for the incident with Square. Apparently, the poor sap in the rear assaulted the girlfriend of one of the Tribe members. In other words, the prick deserved it. If he'd known the bastard had hurt a woman, he'd have volunteered on the spot.

If anyone ever dared touched Stephanie, he'd peel off every piece of their skin with a jagged knife and leave his body out in the heat for the ants to eat…or something else equally agonizing.

Dom shifted in his seat. Where did that come from? She was nothing to him, or so he tried to convince himself. It was a dangerous game he played. Pretending to date her in the hopes that the woman might give up her story and he could save her life. Again.

That was the only reason. Right? She deserved to be happy and he preferred his solitude. It would never work, as much he tried to pretend it was or wasn't something he wanted. There was no place in his life for a woman. Dom pounded a fist on the steering wheel.

As much as he tried to deny it, he liked her, and he didn't care for most people. It was out of character for him but whenever she was around, it seemed normal. He felt like a human being and someone worthy of being in a relationship. Was Roman right? That he was a good man? Dominic ran his fingers through his hair.

Having her pressed up against him last night certainly felt good and was something he'd never experienced before. Not being with a woman but being with, what was the word he was searching for, *the* woman. He cursed under his breath. Was she the one for him? The special someone that could make his life complete? Not since Angelia did he even fathom having someone in his life, and that hadn't ended well. Where did a person even start? What did he know about dating or relationships? He was responsible for the death of the only one he'd ever cared about and there was no way he would go through that again. Couldn't lose someone he loved again.

It was best to keep things casual. Continue to teach her ways to defend herself if he wasn't around. Maybe he'd get her a firearm. Nothing said "I care" more than a handgun and a box of bullets. The sign for the funeral home was up ahead. Anderson's, that's what it was called. Turning off the road, he drove around to the back, hit the button for the garage door opener, and backed inside. The owner stood waiting. Dom didn't know the man's first name, didn't care.

"Hey." Mr. Anderson had shed his suit jacket and wore a short-sleeved dress shirt and tie.

"I have a delivery." Getting out of the van, Dom wished he'd worn his hair up. The back of his neck was soaked. Anderson pulled a gurney over and after Dom opened the back, they each tugged on the body bag until it was in place.

"I can take it from here." The funeral director loaded the stiff onto the conveyor. Once the body was in place, Mr. Anderson flicked the switch that started the fire and set things in motion.

After giving the man an envelope full of cash, Dom drove back to his place. He had the rest of the day off, which was rare. There were several orders for knives he had to do anyway. Who would have ever thought he could make money doing something that he actually enjoyed? Something that didn't involve blood, guts, and rotten flesh. His step was lighter just thinking about it. Working in the shed would be damn hot but at least there was a breeze.

The rest of the day flew by. He'd shed his shirt but not his leather apron. No need to get burned by flying sparks. His body had enough wounds as it was. Despite the orders, he created something else, a ceremonial wedding sword. It must have been Valentina's wedding that inspired it. Lord knew he would never need one. It took him all afternoon but it still wasn't done. The shaft would need some engraving and he'd created a heart-shaped piece to be added below the handle which was wrapped in leather.

Doing his blacksmith work was one of the few things he really loved. It was the only thing from his former life that he still wanted to do. Sure, he created weapons that the family used, and some still were used to get their enemies to talk, but he also did it for the act of creating something that wouldn't be used to destroy something. It was therapeutic, so to speak. Good versus evil and beauty versus ugliness. He hit the blade one more time on a new piece before setting it aside and reaching for the wedding sword. A person had to concentrate or things could go bad in a hurry.

Wiping the sweat from his forehead with the back of his hand, Dom left the shed and admired his work in the daylight. The steel glistened in the sun. It was impressive, if he did say so himself. There was a lot left to do but he set it aside to get one of the easier requisitions done. There was no way he wanted to get behind.

Dom worked another hour. The radio broke in a few times warning that the weather was unstable. What else was new? It'd been crazy all week. The day was humid as hell and very windy.

Glancing at his watch, it was time to finish up and shut everything down. Usually, the thought of quitting when everything was going well would have pissed him off, but he was meeting Stephanie at the gym. Would she be wearing her short shorts and tank top again?

Damn. Dominic shoved his burned fingers into a bucket of water. So much for daydreaming about a woman, he almost scalded his whole hand when he touched the hot metal. That was foolish and something he never did. One minute he was drooling over Stephanie and the next he never wanted to see her again. He liked things to be orderly in his life. She was chaos and fire. Once everything was put away, he walked to the house.

Dom yanked off his clothes as he headed to the shower. The cold water did nothing to erase her from his mind. Stroking himself off as the water beat down on his chest didn't help either. Tonight would be it. He was done. If she didn't give up her story, Roman could do whatever he wanted with the pretty blonde and he wouldn't give a shit.

His life was just fine before she entered it. It was simple, quiet, and didn't involve any women. Enough of the grief. It was a done deal. Donning some workout clothes, he grabbed his keys and left his house. Tonight, he'd give her the tools he thought were most important to survive, ask her one more time to come clean, and then wipe his hands of the whole thing.

As he walked into the gym and saw Jasper showing her some kicks and jabs, the whole thought process went out the door. It shouldn't aggravate him that another man had his hands on her, but it did. He let out a low growl. They both eyed him cautiously as if caught in some illicit act.

"I was just showing Steph some kicks and holds until you got here. What took you so long?" Jasper had already worked up a sweat. "We were about to give up."

He was late and he was acting like a dick. Twice he'd decided against coming in the hope that it would just piss her off and she'd never want to see him again but he just couldn't go through with it.

Dominic rubbed his chin. He needed a shave but hadn't gotten around to it. "I had work to do."

"Family business?" Jasper asked, suddenly alert. "What the hell, you should have called me."

"A delivery." Dom dropped his phone and keys on a nearby bench. "Had some orders to finish for the center." He was dressed in shorts and a tee like the other two. Even though it was early June, Stephanie's trim legs were already a honey brown color.

"I can't believe you're a frickin' crafter," Jasper teased.

If it wasn't for the fact that he wanted to get this over and done with, he'd have challenged the man over what he considered an insult.

"He's an artisan. Have you seen what he's

created? They are masterpieces, every one of them," Stephanie spoke up.

It was a toss-up who was more shocked at her defense. Jasper rolled his eyes. Dominic's face flushed. No one but the Caponellis had ever defended him before.

"Let's get on with it." Dominic brushed the comment aside. He had a job to do and then it was time to get her to confess and go home alone. For the next two hours, he and Jasper sharpened Stephanie's defense mechanisms. Before long, Steph could predict when she might expect a hit next and where to strike first. She'd never be able to take down the two of them in a fight, but if two unsuspecting guys were to attack, she'd at least have a fighting chance. The woman was no wimp and learned fast.

By ten, they were all sweating and tired. Dominic and Stephanie each sat on a bench. Dom drank water and Steph dabbed at her face and neck with a towel.

"Hey, I've got to get going. I've got a date." Jasper grabbed his bag and waved. "Night." An awkward silence followed his departure.

Dominic grabbed for a nearby towel. "So, have you thought any more about sharing your past?"

"No, so you can forget about pretending to be my new boyfriend for information. It isn't happening." Stephanie marched off to where her purse lay. "I know you kissed me and it was amazing but…"

It was on the tip of his tongue to deny it, but could he? "Steph."

"What?" She put both fists on her hips. "I don't trust people and I don't trust you. I will be forever grateful for what you did for me but I can't fall for someone who isn't going to be there to catch me. Are you that man?" She stared him in the face and he looked to the ground. "Others have said they were and then they turned around and did things to me that destroyed my life." Was there a former boyfriend stalking her? "Well, are you?" she asked again.

His fists tightened just thinking about someone hurting her but he remained silent.

"For the last few years all I've done is run, but you know what? I don't have anywhere else to go. If they come for me here, I'm going to be ready, but the one thing I don't need is more false promises. From you or anyone." Stephanie tossed her towel to the side.

"Tell me who these people are. Who was Handlebar?" He rested his elbows on his knees.

She rose and paced back and forth a few times. A battle waged itself in her head based on the expression on her face. Finally, she stopped in front of him. Despite working out with the two of them for the past few hours, she still smelled amazing.

"He's part of a California biker club. I witnessed something that they did. Something horrible. I could put them all away." She knelt in front of him and whispered. "That's why they want to put me away."

Her confession stabbed him in the heart. She was vulnerable and an easy target, yet she'd been able to stay hidden for a long time. "Tell me what you saw."

Stephanie jumped as two young guys entered the gym. It was a couple of kids with *Genoa High School* printed on the front of their shirts.

"Let's go." With any luck, she would spill her guts at her apartment and they could finally get the answers Roman demanded.

Stephanie had walked to the gym but now sat in the passenger seat of his truck. She was silent but on edge. Her hands shook and she fidgeted in her seat. As soon as he parked, Steph was out of the truck and sprinting across the street. Dominic flew out of the truck and grabbed her before she could hit the sidewalk.

With an arm around her shoulder, he walked her back to his vehicle where the door stood open. "Just calm down. It will be all right. We can protect you."

"But who will protect you?" Her eyes held tears.

He thought he could be cold but her tears melted the ice around his heart. Dominic took her hands in his. "It will be all right."

Dominic enfolded her in his arms.

A wall of heat hit them both as her apartment building exploded behind them.

Chapter Sixteen

Stephanie

In a flash, everything she had in the world was gone. Well, everything that wasn't in her car. Just when it seemed like things might be getting better in her life, something like this had to happen. If it weren't for Dominic holding her up, she'd have probably sunk to her knees.

"How could this happen? Do you think anyone was inside?" Her face burned and her eyes ached from the flames. What if she'd been home? Her head spun. Despite the already hot and humid night, she shivered.

"I don't know." Dominic pulled her tighter to his chest. "It's too out of control for the firefighters to go in."

After the explosion, the police were there in a matter of minutes, but since the fire department was all volunteers, that took a bit longer. The old building cracked and snapped as flames ate it from the inside out.

"Did you see anyone odd today? Anyone hanging around who shouldn't be here?" Danny, the lone female on the Genoa police force, had just walked up beside them. She'd been first on the scene but ever since backup had arrived, the task of finding out what caused the fire had fallen to her.

"No. I left early in the morning and then hung out with Dom and Jasper at the gym tonight." It was hard not to miss the slight smile on the officer's lips when Steph mentioned Jasper. "After work, I stopped to change. I threw my laptop and purse in the car but then at the last minute, I decided to jog to the gym. Thankfully, I at least have those."

"Did you run home as well?" Danny's gaze wandered to the crowd. Stephanie had seen a news show on arsonists once. After the fire was set, the guilty one usually stayed around to watch it burn.

"No, Dom brought me home." He'd loosened his embrace but still kept an arm around her shoulder. It just dawned on her. Dom wasn't known for being a touchy-feely kind of guy yet he hadn't loosened his hold since the place lit up.

"That so? And where did Jasper go?" She tapped a pen on her chin.

Where did he go? The guy said he had a date but she didn't want to mention that to the officer. A chill went down her arm and she automatically leaned toward Dom. "I have no idea. I have no reason to think he's here. Probably went home." Stephanie glanced at Dom and he just shrugged his shoulders.

"What about scents? Smell anything weird around the building?" Danny was all business.

"Yeah." This time it was Dominic who spoke up and both women turned his way. "Each time I was there I smelled rotten eggs at the top of the stairs."

"Yes, at first I thought it was just a dead mouse or something," Stephanie remembered. "It's only been in the last month but it got worse in the last week. It did smell kind of like rotting eggs or a gas leak." What if there was something seriously wrong and she'd never contacted anyone about it? "Do you think that might be the cause of the explosion?"

"I can't say at this time. That will be up to the fire inspector." The radio blared on Danny's shoulder and she answered it. She started to walk backward. "Look, I have to go. If you think of anything else, you know where to find me."

"Hey, Danny?" Stephanie stepped toward her and the woman stopped. "Was there anyone inside?" She held her breath.

"According to the super, the apartments were all vacant right now except for yours and one in the back corner on the second floor." There were eight apartments, so it was odd that so many were empty.

Dominic rubbed his forehead with his finger. "The one where the smell came from." It was stated as a fact, not a question.

"Appears so." A dispatcher called on the officer's radio again. "Do you have a place to stay Steph?"

"I, uh…" With all the chaos, that was the last thing on her mind. She was still adjusting to the fact that she'd survived death again but the situation remained she was now homeless. Again.

"She has a place." Dominic put an arm around

her waist.

"Okay then." And Danny was gone.

It briefly crossed Stephanie's mind to use one of the self-defense techniques at his possessive hold but she didn't. Dom had done nothing wrong, and as much as Steph didn't want to, it was a given that Madison would let her crash at her place.

She twisted around to face him. "Thanks for everything."

He said nothing but just stared down at her face.

"I'll just get my car and drive to Madison's."

Shouts sounded as firefighters yelled for people to get back and then there was a loud boom. Stephanie watched in horror as her old car blew up. It had just started to leak gas and she hadn't had time to get it fixed. A spark must have caused the explosion, at least she hoped so. It was the only thing she had left. "No. No. No." This time she did fall, and Dom followed her to the ground. He rocked her back and forth, whispering calming words that didn't register but she knew he was there. Would her life always be a nightmare? Later she might cry and break down in tears, but now she was in shock.

Dominic brought her back to her feet. "Let's go." He took her hand and led her to his truck. "You don't need to see any more of this."

Dom's phone beeped and he checked the message. After answering it, he glanced back at the burning building and then stuffed the phone into his pocket. The flames reflected off his face as he opened the driver's door for her to scoot across the bench seat.

"Who was that?"

"Roman."

She jumped in but stayed in the middle. For once in her life, Stephanie had someone beside her and she wasn't ready to distance herself yet. It was too much to take in right now.

"Did he know about the fire?"

"It's all over the news. He can see the flames from his house."

"I can imagine."

The engine roared to life and they waited for an officer to clear the bystanders so they could go down the street. It seemed like everyone was out. A few in the crowd were dressed in pajamas or a robe.

"Is Madison still up?"

"I haven't a clue. She left for Chicago this morning. Her mother fell ill." Dominic maneuvered his large vehicle through the gawkers and parked cars.

"What? I hope it's nothing serious."

"Doesn't sound like it but they're doing some tests tomorrow and she wanted to be there."

"I don't mean to sound selfish, but what do I do now? I was hoping I could stay with her. Where will I go? I have no cash, no money, and no clothes besides what I have on." So much for being strong, panic had set in. At least when she'd left with nothing before she'd had a plan. It never occurred to her that the building she lived in might burn down.

"You're coming home with me." He placed his hand over hers. "And you're staying with me."

"No, you don't have to do this." Her lower lip trembled.

"I do. Like you said, you have nowhere else to go. Tomorrow. you can go shopping."

"I don't care about the clothes, but oh god, my laptop." The tears started. "It had all my stories on it."

"You had a backup, right?" Dominic drove them out of town.

"Yes, but laptops cost money. I have no insurance so I've lost everything."

"We'll go to the bank in the morning."

"You don't understand." She was on the verge of hysterics now and kept rattling on and on. "I couldn't open a bank account without the proper ID. Madison paid me in cash. It was all in my apartment. All my money is ash right now. Gone. It's all gone."

Dominic pulled over to the side of the road and framed her face with his hands. "Look at me. I know you don't care for Roman, but you are family because of Madison. You will always be taken care of." He brushed his thumb across her chin. "I will take care of you."

His eyes bore into hers. Even if she had any life left in her right now there was no use fighting with the man. It was a done deal so no use disagreeing. Her options were next to none.

"Everything will be okay. You will be okay. Do you understand me?"

All she could do was nod and he wiped her tears away with his thumb.

The phone in his pocket buzzed again but he didn't move.

"You'd better take that."

Dominic dropped one hand but kept the other on her cheek. An odd expression came over his face as he read the message. "It's from Roman."

"What is it?" Nothing would surprise her now. What else could happen?

Dominic handed her the phone and put the truck back in gear. Staring back on the screen was a picture of the two them outside of the fire. The *Genoa Globe* had taken their photo.

They looked like a young couple in love. Dominic's arm was wrapped around her protectively. The headline read: *Young Couple Lose Possessions in Fire but Still Have Each Other*. Looking closer, she could see it had been shared more than a thousand times already. Roman's text said they'd gone viral. Everyone loved a tragic story with hope, but right now she had none.

Taking a deep breath, Stephanie sat back in the seat. Exhaustion hit hard. "I don't even have a car to get to work. With Madison gone, who will work?"

His phone buzzed again and he handed it to her. "Can you check that for me?"

"You trust me to check your messages?" She raised an eyebrow. He'd always been a private person but she did it anyway.

"I don't text and drive. The last thing I need is to have an accident when I have a stiff in the back."

She shivered and unconsciously glanced in the back. He wouldn't be driving around with a body in the bed of his truck, but if he had the work van, that might be a different story.

The phone buzzed again. It was a text from Madison.

Tell Steph I send my love and get some rest.

Stephanie answered.

Hi, Maddy. It's Stephanie. Thanks.

I'll be home soon. Whatever you need is yours.

Thanks.

Roman and I told Dom to take good care of you.

She bet they did.

She turned the phone off. He'd been ordered to take care of her. How did one answer that— "Thanks for ordering the man I fantasize about to look after me"? She rolled her eyes. Had he been ordered to hold her like he did? Dom was fishing for answers, that was for sure. Steph slid over into the passenger seat, needing some distance.

"Everything all right? Who was it?"

"It was Maddy. She sends her love."

"That's good."

Silence followed and she rested her head against the window. She'd been to his place in the country before. It was a small log cabin by the lake but still close to town. They were almost there.

After turning off the road, he parked next to his home. Steph jumped out of the truck and hurried to the water. Crickets and bullfrogs chatted in the moonlight. It was peaceful and calming, just want she needed.

Dominic didn't need to say anything. She knew he was beside her. For how many years now had she wished there was someone in her life to comfort her in trying times—but not out of obligation.

"Are you helping me because you were ordered to?" Stephanie needed to know. Madison was the only person she trusted of the Caponelli crew.

"No." He stopped in front of her. Blocking the view of the lake, he ran his fingers through his hair. "Roman wants you dead."

She gasped and stepped back. "What?" Did she hear him right? What did he have against her? "What the hell are you talking about?" She'd just lost everything she had in the world and now someone wanted to kill her. Was that why she was here? It was hard to catch a breath.

"He wants you dead," Dom reaffirmed.

No. God, no. Her heart dropped to her knees and she tried to focus. It all made sense now, yet it didn't. She'd done everything to stay alive only to be killed by a lake at the request of her boss's husband. Dominic was the Caponelli cleaner. She took a step back. He'd brought her here to kill her, and the fire just eliminated everything she had. It would be as if she never existed, and very soon she wouldn't.

Chapter Seventeen

She turned to run but he grabbed her arm. "Where are you going?"

"If you think I'm going to just stand here and let you kill me, you've got another think coming." Stephanie put her fists up. She wasn't going down without a fight. Exhaustion was setting in but her resolve was strong.

"What? You think I brought you here to kill you?" Even in the dark, the shock could clearly be seen on his face.

"I guess the fire wasn't enough," she mocked. "What, did someone forget you were taking me on a so-called date?" Her eyes narrowed and her jaw twitched. Of all the stupid things for her to blurt out even if it wasn't true, she was vulnerable and out here alone with him. "I can't believe I fell for it. Fell for your stupid words. What an idiot I am." Her eyes watered.

"No, you've got this all wrong." He stepped back and shook his head. "I didn't bring you here to kill you. Calm down."

"But you just said that he wants me gone. Dead." A chill ran down her arm and she drew a finger across her neck. "Now why in the hell would he do that?"

"He's afraid you're a threat to the family, to Madison. She's the only reason you're still alive."

"I don't understand," she choked out. "What have I done? And what about all that talk about being part of the family because of Madison."

"You are and you've done nothing wrong. It's just Roman." Dominic shrugged. "He takes anything he sees as a threat seriously."

She dropped her hands. *That jerk.* "I've never liked him. I knew he was mafia the minute I saw him."

"Now how would you know he's a made man?" His eyebrow lifted.

It was on the tip of her tongue to tell him. That she'd grown up surrounded by them. That it was the only family she'd ever known.

"I've seen movies," Stephanie bluffed, and he scoffed. The man didn't seem to buy it for one minute. "But that still doesn't explain why he has an issue with me."

Dominic let out a deep sigh. "Roman likes to know everyone and everything that goes on in town." He paced. "He doesn't know you. We don't know you. Who you are or where you come from. If he knew about what happened with Handlebar..." Dominic shook his head and looked to the sky. "What happened in his wife's store...holy shit. We'd both be dead."

Stephanie frowned as that settled in. He had as

much to lose as she did. Did she have a partner in crime? Someone who might be on her side for once?

"Do you understand me now?" Dom stepped in front of her. Roman would blow a fuse if he knew what had happened, and Dominic was walking a fine line keeping that info from him.

"I know, I know." She fidgeted with her hair. "But the fire? Did he do that? Did he blow my place up?"

He shook his head. "No. We don't know who did it, but my guess is a meth lab blew. I had my suspicions about it and it was stupid of me to not take it seriously. You could have been killed."

"What?" One of her neighbors had a meth lab?

"Jasper just sent me a text that the tech guys confirmed that the drug dealers we were looking for had moved their operation there recently. Might be why the others who lived there had moved out. They knew something you didn't. I just wish we'd known this sooner."

"Oh my god." She twisted a piece of hair around her finger. "That's scary to think I could have been passing a drug dealer in the hallway every day and not even known it."

Dominic stood staring down at her. His face was full of shadows in the moonlight.

"What am I going to do?" Things were spiraling out of control. She'd become complacent and comfortable in Genoa. "I have nothing and no one. And my boss's husband wants me dead." What else could go wrong? She didn't have anywhere else to go and it wasn't too long ago that she was determined to stay. It was surprising how one thing could throw a person's whole life up in the air.

A knot formed in her stomach. All the self-defense classes in the world couldn't fix this. Stephanie truly was alone and she wouldn't wish that on anyone. Now she was out in the middle of nowhere with the only person who seemed to want to help. He may have been spreading it on a little thick earlier trying to get the truth from her, but Dominic could be trusted. She'd wanted their date to be real for so many reasons, but right now the last thing she needed was to care about anyone. Right now, she didn't want to feel anything. She was empty.

"You stay with me." Dominic's voice echoed in the night.

"Because you're ordered to keep an eye on me? What happens when Roman orders you to kill me? Is that why you took me on a 'date'? To get more info?" She picked up a rock, walked to the shore, and threw it in the lake. A pop sounded when it fell through the surface.

He snapped a twig as he moved behind her. Dominic pushed her hair to one side and placed a hand on each shoulder. She shivered and he drew her closer. Heat radiated off his skin and he smelled like pine. A bullfrog croaked somewhere along the lake.

This wasn't like him from everything that she'd heard. The man avoided relationships of any kind, but right now he was her only hope. Her only protector.

Dominic tightened the hold he had on her and

then he turned her around. She placed a hand on his broad chest. His heart beat strongly beneath her palm.

"That will never happen. I promise you." He tucked a piece of loose hair behind her ear.

"But what if it does? Will you be the one who will take my last breath?" Her voice shook. So many emotions waged inside her.

"No." His deep voice sent a chill down her spine.

"How can you say that?" This evening had turned into a nightmare for her. She'd lost her car, her apartment, and all her money. Now her life dangled in the wind like a broken tree limb.

"No one will ever hurt you. I won't let them." He tipped her chin with his finger.

"Why?" A tear fell down her cheek. "Why would you do that?"

"I will protect you." His hands rested on each side of her neck. His breathing as labored as hers. If only it was true, but right now she didn't believe anyone.

"Why?" This made no sense. He was a loner. Didn't date, didn't care about anyone but the Caponellis, yet he would take her side against them?

"Because."

Through the tears, she laughed. That was no excuse at all. Would no one give her a damn straight answer?

"Because why?" She wanted to know where she stood. What was his game?

Dominic remained silent. From the expression on his face, a mixture of emotions seemed to be struggling it out in his head.

She just shook her head and started to walk back to his truck. Maybe she could stay with Danny.

"Where are you going?" Dominic yelled.

"If you think I'm staying here with you when I have no idea what's going on in your brain, you have another think coming. I'll walk back to town."

"Wait. Don't go."

Stephanie reached his vehicle and leaned against the cool metal of the truck. "Then tell me why you are protecting me from your boss."

Dominic let out a deep breath, ran his fingers through his hair, and cursed under his breath

"I'm waiting." She narrowed her eyes. "I'm out of here." Stephanie turned and he grabbed her by the arm.

"Because I want you for myself." He stepped in front of her and crushed his lips to hers like he did the other night under the street lamp. As crazy as it seemed, ever since she first laid eyes on him, she'd wanted him, wanted the cleaner for the mob. She was as messed up as he was. The life she'd run from was about to swallow her up again, but right now that didn't matter. Nothing mattered except this moment.

The kiss was just as rousing as the last one. It wasn't surprising, because Dominic did everything with intensity, with passion, with mystery. His arm tightened around her waist and he pulled her closer. It was a good thing as she'd probably fall over if he wasn't keeping her upright. His mouth worked magic on hers. This wasn't a sweet kiss. It was a possession. His heart beat fiercely against her chest.

Every finger of his hand burned a print upon her back. He tasted of coffee and sweets. He tasted like home.

When his lips left hers, she whimpered. Dominic rested his forehead against hers for a moment. "Come, let's go inside." He took a step back. His hand was held out for her to take but she couldn't move. Her gaze was glued to his extended palm.

"No, I can't." She was too vulnerable right now to be inside and alone with him.

"You can and you will." His voice calm, as if trying to coax a pet to come to his master.

Her lip quivered and she shook her head. Stephanie looked into his eyes. He must have read it as fear, as his face softened.

"You need rest." Dominic took her hand in his. "You sleep in the bed. I'll stay on the couch."

Her head tilted to the side. She really was too tired to stay upright. If he did try anything, she'd be too worn out to fight. "You swear?"

"You have my word."

She was exhausted. Stephanie finally nodded and followed him to the cabin.

Dominic didn't say another word as he flipped the light on. It was cool inside and hadn't changed any from the last time she was here. Despite being rustic, the place had central air. Dominic walked over to the kitchen and grabbed a bottle of whiskey from the shelf. After pouring a couple fingers into the glass, he placed it on the counter in front of her. "Drink." From the look on his face, he wasn't up for any arguing.

The dark liquid burned as it went down but it did

warm her from the inside. When she finished, he motioned toward the bedroom. "Take a shower if you want. Towels are in the closet. If you need anything, let me know." He leaned against the sink. His eyes said it all. She may have doubted his intentions but it was obvious he did care. He did have feelings for her even if he totally didn't understand them himself. No one would get to her tonight. She had a warrior standing guard. Tomorrow, in the light of day, things may be different, but right now she was safe. Home.

***

Dominic

Letting her go off to his bed alone was one of the hardest things he'd ever done. Stephanie had always been pretty to him, but looking vulnerable and exposed like she did tonight was breathtaking. Did that make him a monster to want to prey on that helplessness? So be it. He'd been too long without a woman and she called to him like no one ever did.

Even taking her in his arms was both heaven and hell. He wanted to crush her to him, hold her tight. To feel her soft skin against his. To inhale that beautiful scent of flowers that followed her everywhere. She hadn't resisted the kiss, which had his heart soaring and his dick as hard as nails.

It puzzled him to no end that she might want him. Most women just wanted the thrill of being with a killer, a bad boy to tell their friends about, but she seemed to see something in him that others didn't. Stephanie was a good person. He knew it in his heart. She was defenseless and in trouble. The fact was she deserved better than him, but Stephanie had no one else. Was that why she didn't resist? There was no one to defend her but him. He'd always avoided relationships. They made one weak, but all he felt right now was strength and the determination to protect her with his life. He was her last hope and she was his. If he ever dreamed of having a woman again, it was now. Maybe it was time to bury the past before it buried him.

Being his woman may put her at risk, but from what he could tell, he was the least of her worries. She'd been running from something scarier than being with him and he was determined to find out what it was.

Dom sent off a text to Jasp, asking him to come up to his place. Carefully, he placed the glass Stephanie drank from into a paper bag. If she wasn't going to tell him who she was, her fingerprints would. The squeak of pipes sounded as Stephanie turned the water on in the bathroom. He gripped the counter just thinking about her standing where he stood just this morning, all naked and wet.

His phone buzzed. Jasper would be there soon and it was a good thing. Dominic quietly slipped out the door and ran down the road. It felt good to be outside. He could still smell smoke on his clothes and he would need a shower also. Maybe he'd just jump in the lake, anything would be better than being that close to the woman that he craved worse than ice cream on a hot summer day.

The lights from Jasper's vehicle were up ahead.

He slowed and walked the last few yards.

Jasper stood waiting. "She all right?"

"As much as can be expected. Was it what we thought?"

"Yeah. Looks like meth heads blew themselves up. Dumbasses. At least we don't have to worry about them anymore." Jasper was dressed in a nice shirt and pants. Probably going on a late-night date just like he said.

"I need you to take this to Roman."

"What the hell is it?"

"Stephanie's fingerprints on a glass so be careful with it."

"Why?" Jasper's mouth dropped open and Dom shared as much as he could. "No shit?"

"Yeah." Dom handed him the paper bag. "How long do you think this will take?"

"Not long hopefully." He placed it on the front seat of his car. "Madison called and had her housekeeper gather a few of her clothes for Steph to borrow until she can get some of her own."

Jasper pulled a tote bag out of the passenger seat. It had some fancy logo on the side. The bag alone probably cost more than everything the woman back at his home ever had.

"Thanks." She'd be happy to have those. Hell, he didn't have anything that would come close to fitting her.

"Oh, and when Maddy heard she'd lost her laptop, she had me get one of those also."

"Where the hell did you get one of those this late?" he asked, though he had a good guess.

"The tech guys." He handed Dom the backpack

containing her new computer.

"Just tell her to log on to her cloud and download everything she had." Jasper caught his gaze and looked him straight in the eye. "Then we can track anything she does. If needed."

If felt like an invasion of privacy but he brushed it off as doing it for her own good. What she didn't know wouldn't hurt her.

Jasper rounded the car and opened the driver's door. "Between the computer and the fingerprints, we should figure out her story soon."

"Yeah." Dominic looped the bags over his shoulders. "If you hear anything, can you let me know? First?" It was a risk, but if he had to get her out of here in a hurry, Dominic would need a head start.

"You know I can't do that." The man frowned. "But if I hear anything, you'll be a quick second."

Dom scowled. He'd known the answer before he said it but had to ask anyway. "Thanks." Jasper's tires spun up dirt as he left. Dominic turned and walked back to the house, a few mosquitoes buzzing around him.

It was quiet when he walked in the door. He put the backpack on the kitchen counter and carried the bag of clothes to the bedroom. The door was open and he peeked in. It was a kick to the gut seeing her lying in his bed. A sight he never dreamed of seeing, never had any hope of witnessing. He knocked but she didn't move.

Dominic walked to her side. She was sound asleep and wearing one of his t-shirts. It was the most beautiful sight he'd ever seen. He pulled the covers over her shoulders and tucked her in. It felt right having her here. As much as he tried to fight it, he wanted her in his life. She was where she belonged and he was keeping her.

Chapter Eighteen

Stephanie

She yawned and stretched like a cat. The mattress was warm, firm, and, she realized with a start, much nicer than her own. With a groan, she rolled over in bed. Dominic's bed. Slowly opening one eye, she took a good look at her surroundings. The nightmare of last night flooded her brain but she pushed it aside. She'd think of that another day. It was just too much at one time.

He hadn't joined her in the night, but then Dom said he wouldn't. It was both a relief and a disappointment. Snuggling into the pillow, she could smell him. It was a combination of the musky sweet smell of the outdoors and his soap from the shower.

His bedroom was just like the rest of the place, simple, sparse, and definitely showed a lack of a woman's touch. There were no pictures on the walls and the curtains were for privacy and shade, not décor. There was a book by the bedside. She picked up the popular thriller. His worth jumped up a notch when she spied he used a bookmark instead of marking his last read spot with a folded over corner. People who did that were not true book lovers. You didn't mar the landscape of nature and you didn't defile the pages of someone's hard work.

The room was empty of furniture except for the bed, a dresser with a mirror, and a bookcase. Curiosity got the best of her and she padded on bare feet over to check out the other books in his collection. There were more thrillers, crime novels, and a few of the classics. Goosebumps rose and she rubbed her arms to stay warm. Peeking in the closet, she found a plaid flannel shirt to slip on. It dwarfed her, to say the least.

The only personal touch in the place were a couple photographs on the dresser. Afraid to touch them, she bent over to study them first. It was a family photo. Dominic's? The photo showed a happy couple with a young boy. The son had Dom's eyes and the father in the photo seemed to share a similar jawline. The mother had a softness to her face that Stephanie had only seen a few times in Dominic when he smiled. It felt like prying to examine it any more.

The other photo was of a young woman, perhaps in her early twenties. She was beautiful with long dark hair, brown eyes, and a wide smile on her face. Her eyes shone with love. Had Dominic taken the picture? Was this a former love? Jealousy spiked out of nowhere at the thought. The photo was obviously old. If he was involved with someone, Madison and Valentina would have known about it.

She pushed the idea of Dom with another woman aside just as she did the other troublesome thoughts. There were other things she needed to deal with first.

Her stomach growled, and after using the bathroom to wash her face, Stephanie carefully opened the bedroom door. Heavy breathing could be heard from the couch. Dominic was obviously in deep sleep. She came to a halt when he came into view. The man had shed his clothes from last night and only wore a pair of charcoal boxer briefs. He was too big for the couch and one foot rested on the ground. His hair was wild and covered part of his face.

She took a step closer. The man was tall and lean but she'd never seen him with so few clothes on. He was the perfect male specimen—tan, strong, and full of muscles—but just as scarred as he was internally, he was on the outside as well. The wood floor creaked as she stepped closer. She covered her mouth with a hand. His entire body was marred with scars. Some appeared to be cuts, some were burns, and some were from God only knew what.

He had a tattoo on his side but she couldn't make out what it was. Stephanie stood transfixed, watching the rise and fall of his chest. The man did things to her that just couldn't be explained. Before she could even blink, he reached out and pulled her to the couch next to him. Her back pressed tightly to his chest and he drew the blanket over them both. She couldn't speak, could barely breathe.

"It's early." The warmth from his breath tickled the back of her ear. "Rest."

It didn't seem possible but in only a few minutes she was fast asleep again.

***

The smell of coffee was in the air. Stephanie snuggled into the blankets for the second time that morning, only this time she awoke on the couch. Alone. Sitting up, she turned to see Dominic leaning against the counter staring at her while sipping the brew from a white mug she recognized from the art center. He was sexy as hell and she probably looked like a sloppy mess.

Her fingers got stuck in the tangles of her hair. Where the hell was her comb? What was the use? Stephanie's whole life was a disaster and the fact that she was homeless and didn't even own the shirt on her back came rushing in. She lay back down and covered her head with the throw.

"Get up." Dominic gently shook her and pulled the cover from her face.

He now had a mug in each hand. She slowly sat up and reached for the one he offered. Dominic sat his on a nearby table and settled in behind her, his long legs on each side of hers. Slowly, he began to work the tangles from her hair with a comb, starting at the bottom and working his way up. Tears welled up in her eyes. No one had ever combed her hair except for her mom when she was a child. It brought memories of childhood with a mother who passed away too young and it brought promises of what could be with this man.

Dominic may have been a monster to some but

he'd come to her rescue more than once, and that was something no one had ever done.

"You're pretty good at this," she managed to choke out.

"I can't dance but I've had a lot of practice with hair."

His fingers touched the back of her neck and she fought the urge to lean back against his chest. Just the warmth from his thighs had her flesh buzzing.

"I heard you don't date either."

"Why, are you interested?" The comb stilled before attacking her twisted strands again.

"Could be." She placed a hand on his thigh. "I need a protector and you seem to be pretty good at that."

"You would sell yourself for a bodyguard?" He laughed. "Last night you thought I was going to kill you. You yourself said you didn't trust me."

"Maybe I changed my mind." Stephanie closed her eyes. He was a dangerous man, yet with him, she really did feel safe. Dominic made her feel things that she thought were dead. The man behind her gave her hope. In all her dealings with him, he'd always treated her with respect and care. Maybe it was time to start living instead of running. "It'd only be selling if I didn't want you and you didn't want me."

"I never said I didn't want you." He flipped the finished side of her hair in front of her shoulder and started on the other. "It's not safe to be with one of us though. You know how Madison's life has changed. She rarely gets to go anywhere alone."

"I don't want to be alone anymore." It was the

truth and it hurt to admit it. She was used to being by herself, but it didn't mean she wanted to be that way forever. It wasn't living, she barely existed.

Dominic sighed and tossed the comb on the couch. "When I was younger, I had a girlfriend. Thought I was in love and all that shit."

"Is that the woman in the photo in your bedroom?"

"Yes."

"You must still care or you wouldn't have her picture."

"No, it's a reminder. Men killed her to get to me."

A gasp escaped her lips as she turned to face him. "I'm so sorry."

"They did horrible things to her. Torture, rape..." He looked away and shook his head. "Having someone to love makes a person weak and they become a target."

"What if the one you care about already is a target? There isn't a doubt in my mind that if the people I am hiding from find me, they will do all of those things as they ultimately want to kill me. At least I will have someone on my side. I know Roman wants me dead too but...I'm not a threat to him. You have to make him believe that. You once said I owed you." Dominic turned her way and looked into her eyes. "I will give you anything you want. Please let me stay. I don't want to run anymore." She really did care for this man. More than she ever thought she would or could.

Strong arms pulled her to his chest and he stroked her hair. "You don't owe me anything. You don't have to run and you can stay as long as you want."

"I don't have anything to offer. I have no clothes, no makeup, shoes, nothing."

"I'll take you shopping and you can get whatever you need. Madison's housekeeper picked out some things and sent them over last night. You were already asleep when they arrived. And Jasper got you a laptop. It's all set to go."

"A what?" She sat up. It was the one thing she missed more than anything. All her hard work had just gone up in smoke.

"A computer to replace the one you lost."

"I know what a laptop is, but seriously? They got me one?" This whole situation was so confusing. One minute the family wanted her dead and the next they were being overly generous.

"Yeah. He said to just go to your backup site and you can get back to your writing."

"I can't believe it." A little hope peeked through the clouds and brightened her day.

"I know you think you lost everything but you have a home here. People who do care." Dom rubbed his leg against hers. Whether it was on purpose or not, it sent tingles down to her toes.

"Do you care?" Her lower lip quivered. Willingly or not, they'd danced around each other for over a year now. Ever since he'd shown up to fix the mess in the shop, Dom had been there whenever she needed him. That wasn't coincidence. It was fate, karma, destiny. But did he feel the same way?

"Yes. I do." His voice was low and raspy.

"Why?" As much as she hoped, there was still that doubt in her mind that he really didn't mean it. Would she ever get over her distrust after what happened with Maksim?

Dominic rubbed the back of his hand against his chin. The scrape of his dark whiskers sent butterflies across her stomach. How she yearned to feel their rough texture against her skin. Her cheeks flushed as she raised her gaze to meet his.

"Why? Because I was truthful when I said ever since I kissed you, I can't get you out of my mind. I try to fight it but I can't."

They stared into each other's eyes for a moment before she laid her cheek on his chest. His heart beat strong against her ear. "Don't fight it and I promise not to run."

"It's a deal." He kissed the top of her head and stroked her hair.

She could move but didn't want to. For the first time in a long time she felt safe, and she was staying right where she was.

***

Maksim

"Hey, boss, you need to see this."

"Can it wait? I'm a little busy right now." Maksim studied the latest request for girls that had just arrived. His clients were getting more and more demanding. The heat was on from the feds also. One had just shown up yesterday questioning the disappearance of a former maid who had worked in the neighborhood. He'd never pulled one that close before but he'd gotten greedy and the price was right.

"No, it can't." Luis tossed his phone on the desk and Maksim picked it up to take a closer look.

It couldn't be, but it was. He'd know that hair and face anywhere. The news article had included a surprisingly good picture of the couple in front of a burning building. The woman was Stassi Bravikova. She was alive.

Chapter Nineteen

Dominic

He'd taken her shopping the next morning. It's was something he hadn't done with a woman in a very long time. She bought a few clothes and toiletries. Stephanie said she didn't want to be indebted to anyone but she didn't have a choice and reluctantly let him pay. After that they went grocery shopping. Something he'd never done with a member of the opposite sex. Surprisingly, it felt nice.

Stephanie continued to stay at his place for the next few days. He was hesitant about their situation at first but they were getting along fine. Madison told her to take the week off to get her wits about her and rest. It was a good thing because Dom knew Roman was pressuring his wife to fire her. Madison's seamstress was filling in until Madison returned next week since her mother had started feeling better.

Stephanie was writing nonstop. He hadn't a clue

what she was working on but it seemed to make her happy. Dominic continued to spend his nights on the couch with Stephanie sleeping soundly in his bed. The woman was vulnerable and still a bit in shock from losing everything she owned. He may have been a killer but he'd never take advantage of a woman at such a weak moment.

It was a nice surprise to find out she was such an amazing cook. She was great in the kitchen and insisted on cooking and doing a little cleaning to pay for her room and board. It didn't matter to him that he was compensated but it did to her. Having a warm home cooked meal waiting for him after a long day was an odd but welcome experience, to say the least. It was also one he could get used to. Jasper said they would have the fingerprint results Friday, which was tomorrow. He had a job today and planned on taking her with him for two reasons. If she was going to be with him, she had to know what she was getting into and he also didn't want to leave her alone.

They'd just gone for a run around the less touristy part of the lake. After a quick shower, unfortunately separately, he had Stephanie riding shotgun in the work van. It was a simple pick up. A clean and go, as he called it. The sun beat down through the window as he drove. Damn, it was hot. There was a good chance a storm was brewing and it would be a bad one. All week it had been in the nineties, with the humidity making it off the charts.

"Where are we going?" She rubbed her arms and he turned down the AC.

"I have a job."

Out of the corner of his eye, he could see her still. "What kind of job?"

"You'll see." It was now or never. She had to see the real him and what he did.

Taking his eyes off the road, he witnessed her slump in the seat. Her pretty lips pouted and her arms crossed in front of her chest. What was she thinking? Stephanie was smart. Sharper than she let others think. He'd noticed that right away. Dominic also suspected she had a connection to a crime family, something older than her association with the Caponellis. She knew too much about the family dynamics and aspects of the business to have just gained that from watching television shows or movies.

It took about thirty minutes to reach the shed. The same building they'd worked Square over in not too long ago. The Mayhem Tribe had found the people responsible for trafficking drugs through town and for blowing up the apartment building where Stephanie had lived. Apparently, the drug dealers had the place wired to blow if the police found out about them. They'd been tipped off, only it wasn't the cops that were on to them but the biker gang.

As they pulled off the road and into the driveway, he spied a couple of the gang members outside. One exhaled some smoke and then snuffed out his cigarette on the ground with his heel. He and the others in his group got on their bikes and started down the drive in their direction. Dominic slowed down but the gang just waved and sped up, leaving a trail of dust along the road.

"Who was that?" Stephanie turned in her seat to watch them go.

"Friends of the family." Dominic parked next to the metal shed. "Stay here." He needed to check out the place first. They'd left the doors open, probably to keep the air circulating. In the middle of the floor lay three bodies on a large plastic sheet. There was no blood, so they'd been killed somewhere else and then transported there. They obviously didn't arrive on the back of their bikes, so someone in their gang must have a truck.

A gasp startled him. There was no reason to turn around, he knew who it was.

"What happened here?" Her fingers wrapped around his arm as she stood behind him. "Who are they?" The fact that she didn't start screaming or calling the police was a good sign.

"Bad people."

"Worse than the ones who killed them?" She squeezed his arm and he turned her way.

"Yes." He slipped from her grasp and looked down at her face. "They were the ones who got your friend's son into drugs and were selling around the schools. It was also these guys who blew up your home. If you would have been there, you'd have been killed." He pointed to the bodies on the floor. "They would have killed you. So, yes, they are worse."

Stephanie swallowed and twirled her hair around her finger. "Did you, you know, have anything to do with what happened to them?"

Dominic narrowed his eyes. Stephanie just proved again that she was not naïve to this lifestyle.

She didn't mention Dominic by name in case the place was wired but the place was clean. "No, but I will now. Roman wants his family and the town to be safe, but it was someone else who did this." The Mayhem Tribe took this group out but it was his job to dispose of them. "We just have to make them go away."

Stephanie nodded and stepped back. Not like she was appalled but more like she was just getting out of the way.

"Stay here and I'll back the van in." Dominic hurried to the van, turned it around, and backed it into the shed. Stephanie stood near the open door, probably to breathe some fresh air. When he got out and opened the back of the van, she was by his side again.

"How do we get them in there?" she asked.

Dom's heart skipped a beat. Not only had she not freaked out but she actually said "we." "You're not upset?"

"I should be, but these are bad people. Killers, drug dealers, and who knows what else they've done. Does this make me sick to my stomach? Yes. But if it is them or me? Or you?" She glanced at the bodies and a shiver rippled through her body. "I'd rather it be them. Let's get this done and get out of here."

Dominic tossed her a pair of leather gloves. Fingerprints could still be left at a scene through latex gloves so he only used leather on a job. They would be too big for her but that didn't matter. What mattered was that she was here and helping. She understood that there was evil in the world and sometimes you had to be as bad as them to get rid of it.

Stephanie helped him lay out the body bags, while he rolled the corpses on to them. He had a ramp that pulled out of the back of the van and lay on the floor. If the guys were too big, he had a pulley system. He was strong but he didn't want to lift three hundred pounds of dead weight if he didn't have to. They gathered all the plastic and stuffed that into another bag that would be going to the funeral home to burn also.

Everything went smoothly and they were on the road back to his place in no time. The woman who'd worked so hard by his side was quiet the whole way. As soon as they got home, she went back to typing at her laptop.

He set an iced coffee on the table near where she sat. "Are you ever going to tell me what you're writing?"

"I usually write romances that all have a happy ending."

"Usually?"

Sighing, Stephanie sat back in her chair and looked up at him. "It's about me and what happened to get me where I am today. I want to get everything out of my system and move on. I can't keep hiding." She shrugged. "It will be fiction and I won't use anyone's names."

"Am I in the story?" He stared down at her and her cheeks blushed. The image of his photo in the center of her board came to mind.

"The most recent parts." Her gaze returned to the screen.

"And how does this one end?"

"I guess we'll find out." There was determination in her eyes. Somehow, things had changed with her in the last week. Right after the fire, she was unsure and withdrawn, but now, Stephanie seemed to have recovered from the loss of her place. Was maybe even a little stronger because of it. Sometimes you had to lose everything to find out what you truly needed.

"Can I read it?" It was a sure bet that she would say no but he had to ask anyway. Time was running out and he needed to know what options they had. She brought out the defender in him. He cared about her. Something he said he'd never do again, but some things were worth fighting for.

They'd skirted around each other for the past year, both trying to ignore the other, yet he caught her staring his way every time he dared look in her direction. In the last few days, they'd shared just about every meal and spent every minute of the day together as if they were a couple. He liked being alone yet he couldn't imagine being here without her. She belonged here, with him.

Stephanie still hadn't answered all of his questions. Her fingers toyed with a pen on the table before she slipped it into the jar that held others. "How about I just tell you?" Dominic nodded, too shocked to answer. "I just want to finish it up and then we'll talk. Okay?"

"Yeah." He took a step back. "Yeah, I'll be out in the shed when you're ready."

It was like opening an oven door when he stepped outside. The temperature had to be ninety-six in the shade. It would be a bitch in the shed but it was important that Stephanie finish what she needed to do. After waiting so long to hear what had happened in her life, it would finally be out in the open. Was he ready for it? Nothing she could say would shock him, at least he hoped not. Whatever it was, they would figure things out together.

There was no way he would be welding or starting the hopper this afternoon. Even with all the doors open and the strong breeze, it was still toasty. Dom decided to use the rest of the afternoon to organize his tools and put things away. Before he knew it, the sky had darkened, not from the late hour but from the approaching storm. The radio crackled several times with weather warnings and he could hear the storm siren going off in Genoa.

Dammit, he had better go check on Stephanie. After shutting the doors and turning off the lights, he set off for the house. Lightning flashed and he glanced to where it still lit up the sky over the lake.

He stopped in his tracks. There standing alone on his dock was Stephanie. She was too close to the edge. His heart stopped. Was she going to jump?

Chapter Twenty

Stephanie

The water felt wonderful on her toes. Tossing her shorts and top to the side, she jumped in. Slipping below the water felt heavenly after the hot day. Even the air conditioning in the cabin couldn't keep up. Coming to the surface, she reached for the dock. Out of nowhere, a hand grabbed her and pulled her out of the lake.

"What the hell are you doing?" Dominic yelled.

"Cooling off. It's stuffy inside so I felt like jumping in the water."

"I thought..." He briefly closed his eyes and then seemed to relax. "Are you ready to talk?"

"Yeah, let's go inside." A crack of thunder sounded in the distance but for the first time in forever, it didn't bother her. It was as if she'd been reborn. Purging the words from her mind and then cleansing the heat from her body was like a rebirth.

Dominic poured them each a glass of brandy and then they sat on the couch. It felt like he walked on eggshells, not wanting her to bolt or change her mind, but she was done. Her life started over today and there was no more looking back.

"Is the storm going to bother you?" Thunder was sounding closer.

"Not anymore, but it was what triggered the nightmares." She took a sip of the brandy. It burned as it slid down her throat. His gaze never left hers. "Like I said, I'm from California. I was the daughter of a mob boss."

Dominic nodded as if to verify the confession. He knew she was from their world even if it was the last thing she ever wanted to admit to. "Not just any boss but *the* boss. I thrived on being his only daughter, the princess, so to speak. I grew up very wealthy and anything and everything I wanted was delivered to the complex where I lived. Private schools, rich friends, and expensive cars. I thought of myself as royalty even if no one else did." Twisting, she lifted her hair to show the tattoo on the back of her neck. It was a crown with her initials entwined in it.

"Are those your real initials?" Dominic brushed a thumb across the tattoo and goosebumps rose on her arms.

"Yes. Well, the S was for a nickname." Stephanie let her hair drop and she leaned into the couch. "I considered myself, like I said, a princess, but I wasn't anything. I was just a tool for my father to use to further his ambitions. He contracted me to marry Maksim, the son of a high-ranking member of a rival family. Silly me, I thought of it as romantic and doing my duty."

Dominic remained quiet and unmoving except when she mentioned the contract. He went to interrupt but she shook her head.

"One night, I decided I wanted to have a little fun. Escape my bodyguards and get out of the mansion that I had spent almost all of my time in. I'd found a business card for a new, very private club one of the guards had left lying around. I called my friends from school and we snuck out one stormy night. We had to meet a limo at a secret location, surrender our phones, and then we were taken to the club. But there was no club."

Dominic's fist tightened on his thighs.

"We were surrounded by members of what looked like a biker group. Handlebar was one of them. My friends screamed to be let go and we all had no idea what was happening. Then a man with a mask on came in and looked everyone over. He pointed and said where this one or that one would be taken. I couldn't move yet I was running a hundred miles an hour in my head. It couldn't have been true. Things like that don't happen, but it did. My friends wouldn't be there if it hadn't been for me. Bags were tossed over our heads and I remember the look of fear on Marina's face." She shook her head as the memories flooded back. "I will never forget that as look as long as I live."

"What happened to them? Do you know where they were sent?" Dominic reached for her hands and held them tight.

"No, but they were taken by human traffickers. I'm sure they were out of the country in a matter of hours."

"I'm so sorry. We'll tell Roman and try to find them."

"It's been years." The pain in her heart would never go away but she'd survived. She had to get over the guilt that had been eating her alive for so long. "From what I've read about what happens to these people, I doubt any of them are still alive."

Before she knew it, he gathered her in his arms. His thumb gently traced up and down the back of her neck. "How did you escape?"

"Someone recognized me. After all the others had been led away, I remained there with that hood over my head. They called another man over and someone showed them the tattoo on the back of my neck." She looked him in straight in the eye. "I could see his shoes and I recognized the voice. It was Maksim."

"He was the trafficker? The bastard." Dominic cursed.

"Yes, he was the head of it, and I was to marry this monster." The betrayal, the hurt, the anger, all those memories had been put to words in her novel. Her pain was now shed from her body and onto a page. Sure, she didn't want to marry the man, but he'd lied about everything. She'd had no clue that was what he was into.

"Did he admit it? Say anything to you?"

"No, I was just shoved into the back of a car and sent back to my father. He was furious with me for putting him in that position."

"Your father was mad at you?"

"I begged him to help my friends but he said if anyone inquired about the last time I had seen them,

I was to lie. That I hadn't seen anyone since school. My father took everything away. I had no computer, no newspaper, no TV, nothing that I could check to see where they'd gone. A week later, I overheard a few guards talking and I knew it was hopeless. They said they'd been sent overseas, never to be seen again. I guess their families had searched everywhere and there were rewards but they never found them. After all of that, I was still expected to marry that creep. He made my flesh crawl. I couldn't spend the rest of my life with him; I would die first. But I kept up appearances, waiting for my chance to get out of there."

"So you just left and changed your name?"

"It wasn't that easy. I had help. Al Handy—he worked on the family vehicles. Father didn't trust anyone else as they might add a tracker or bomb. They called him Jeeper because he loved Jeeps and drove one." She smiled thinking of the guy who ended her old life and gave her a new one. "He'd show up every day with this white dog. It looked like a boxer mix, but I don't know what kind it was. It was just a big white dog with a red nose named Willy Dawg."

"He helped you escape?"

"Yes. After that happened, my father forbade me from leaving the place. I even had dress fittings for my wedding at the house. Then one evening, my dad had to leave and took a lot of the men with him. It was some big meeting with the heads of all the other families in the area. They left only a new guy there to watch me."

"That seems odd." Dominic took another drink

from his glass.

"I know. Al knew what happened to me and offered to make me some new IDs. He also gave me a key to a car that would be sitting in a nearby parking lot if I could get away. I packed some clothes and ran out the back door as soon as everyone left."

"That seems a little too easy. Do you think your dad arranged it? You would be free but he'd still save face for the contract?"

That had crossed her mind once or twice. No one wanted to believe a parent would be so cruel as to give their flesh and blood to someone with such a disregard for human life. She searched the papers many times to see if anyone had been searching for her but there was nothing. He either didn't want her back or didn't want to be embarrassed by the betrayal.

"I don't know. I just knew I had to disappear. If Maksim ever found me, I don't doubt for a minute he would kill me. Trafficking probably isn't the only thing he does with that biker gang. Handlebar would have turned me in and I'd be dead. But I couldn't involve Roman. Maksim is from a very powerful family. One you don't want to mess with. I can't trust my father either after what happened."

Dominic seemed to ponder her words. What was he thinking about all of this? Did he question getting involved with her? If they found her, it would put everyone in danger and he'd be smack dab in the middle of everything.

"That's a lot for anyone to handle." He encouraged her. "What made you decide to tell me this now?"

"After my place blew up, I finally came to terms with my life. I didn't want to hide anymore. I wanted to live. If telling my story gets me killed, so be it. I can't live in the shadows anymore. I'm dying a little every day." She'd used a pen name but there was always a chance someone would recognize the characters in her story for who they really were.

"We need to tell Roman. He will know what to do."

"I guess." It might be the best thing to do since she wanted to stay.

"And the storms?" Dominic removed his arm from around her shoulder and took her hand in his.

"They will probably always bring back memories of that night. And seeing Handlebar a couple months ago caused the break down I had the night I was here." A flash of lightning caused the lamps to flicker.

"Do you know how to get rid of bad memories?" He cupped her chin with his palm.

"No." His eyes shone darker than normal and she flushed under his gaze.

"You replace bad memories with good ones." His lips lowered to hers in a gentle kiss. It was first a tender, light kiss that turned into a more passionate one. This man may have had wounds as deep as hers, but in her heart, she knew they were just two lost souls that had been waiting to be united. He tasted of the brandy they shared. He tasted of hope and compassion. He tasted of love. For the first time in a long time, she felt at peace. She felt like she was finally home. She felt loved.

When his mouth left hers, she leaned in for more but he stood up.

"What's wrong?" She'd just bared her life to him and now he was leaving?

"Nothing, but I need to cool off. Take a shower." He took a step and headed toward the bedroom. What the hell was wrong with the man? As if reading her thoughts, Dominic stopped by the door and turned around. "Care to join me?" The wide smile caused her knees to weaken. If she wasn't already sitting down, she'd probably be on the floor.

He stood with his hand out for her. Waiting. If she took it, it would mean only one thing. She'd be his for now and always.

Chapter Twenty-One

"I, uh, yes." Stephanie snapped out of the shock. Dominic wouldn't ask twice so she wasn't about to wait for him to change his mind. When she reached his side, the man pulled her close and caressed her cheek. His eyes were the color of milk chocolate and she leaned in closer. When their lips touched, the lights flickered. Whether it was the storm or their electricity, she didn't know, didn't care.

Dominic was an amazing kisser. Her eyes closed as his lips took sweet advantage of hers. He always seemed to start tenderly, as if fearful she might change her mind. As she relaxed in his arms, his tongue slipped between her lips and he tightened his hold. The evidence of his desire for her pressed hard against her belly.

When his mouth left hers, the room spun. He did that to her both physically and mentally.

"Follow me before I take you up against the wall." He took her hand and pulled her his way.

"Maybe I want you to do that." She pulled back and grinned.

"I have that planned for later." Dominic picked her up in his arms and carried her into the bathroom. "As well as a few other places."

Setting her carefully on the ground, he turned on the water in the shower and tested the temperature. Dom lifted his shirt over his head and threw it on the floor.

"Your turn," he teased, but she was too busy staring at his chest to care. She reached out to touch him but he caught her hand in his. Shaking his head, he reached for the hem of her shirt and eased it off just as easily as he did his.

Standing there under the heat of his gaze was intense, and even though she still had on a bra and shorts, her hands automatically came up to cover herself. Dominic took her hands in his and pulled them behind her back as he dropped light kisses to the top of her shoulder and then worked his way to the top of her breasts. She was giddy with sensation as his whiskers fluttered across her chest.

"Take this off." He didn't say what but she knew he meant everything she had on.

Before she could act, he dropped his pants and got in the shower. All she could do was stare. The man was perfection. As the warm water trickled down his skin, she unconsciously wiped the imaginary drool from her chin.

Shaking the cobwebs from her brain, she unhooked her bra and dropped her shorts. When she looked up, Dominic stood unmoving. Stephanie carefully stepped into the shower and he stepped behind her. The water felt heavenly but not anywhere as good as the man behind her. He held a bar of soap in his hand and began to move it across her skin. Along her spine, across her breasts, and down her legs.

Steam filled the small room along with the citrus smell of the soap. Stephanie tried to keep her hair from getting wet but it was a losing battle. Over the rush of water, thunder rumbled in the distance. After thoroughly cleansing both their bodies, Dominic rinsed them off with the shower head.

As the water trailed down her legs, Dom twisted her around and took her mouth again. He twisted one hand in her hair as he kissed her deeply. She moaned as he tightened the hold around her waist. Ending the sweet assault on her lips, Dominic gazed down at her with half-closed eyes. "We'd better get out. The storm's getting closer."

"What storm?" Stephanie barely noticed it. How could she concentrate on anything other than the intoxicating man holding her close? He turned off the water and held her hand so she wouldn't slip.

A soft, fluffy towel enveloped her as he dried every drop from her skin.

"I'm clean." Dominic turned the towel on himself.

"I sure am." Stephanie blushed.

He laughed. "No, I mean health wise. I've never been with anyone without using a condom."

"Oh, I haven't either." It was that awkward safe sex conversation.

"Are you on the pill?" Dom draped the damp towel over a hook.

"Yes, Madison hooked me up with the family's doctor." She motioned between the two of them.

"We're good."

He stepped closer. Close enough that her breasts were pressed up against his broad chest. "Good, because I don't want anything to ever come between us."

"I don't either." She placed her hand on his heart. It beat strong and just as wildly as hers.

"If we do this, you belong to me." The Caponelli crew were all the same way. Intense, demanding, and loyal. Roman would give his last drop of blood to protect and keep Madison, and it would be the same with this man.

"I already do." As much as she fought it, he was under her skin, in her soul. He was dark to her light and together they were complete.

This time his kiss was filled with passion and love. Something that neither of them had had much of in their lives. Something she was eager to make up for. The lights flickered again and Dominic took her hand and led her to the bed. He was being gentle with her, she could tell. Probably calmer than he wanted to be, and it warmed her heart even more.

As she settled into the center of the bed, the onslaught of light kisses continued. The whisker rubs along her neck drove her crazy. His hair trailing along her skin as he went. When his lips touched her hip and continue farther, her hips bucked off the sheets. He held her tight as his mouth tormented her where no man had before. Licking, sucking, and creating havoc within her soul. It was too much and over too quickly as the most intense orgasm of her life rippled through her.

Crawling back up her body, he framed her face

with his hands. "You're so beautiful. It makes my heart ache."

Who would have thought this man could be so tender and sweet? An overwhelming contentment filled her, but that wasn't to last. His hands moved to her breasts, caressing the globes before lowering his mouth to her nipples. She swallowed as her head moved from side to side on the pillow as he teased the nubs to tight peaks.

Dominic's hand stimulated the bud between her legs and she was on fire again. He could've spent hours tormenting her like this but he'd reached his threshold. Pushing her legs farther apart, he settled between her thighs. Gazing into her eyes, he filled her with one thrust. Her eyes closed as an overwhelming feeling of love filled her heart.

Slowly, they moved as one, but soon he took over, moving harder and faster. Blood rushed in her ears, the muscles in her thighs tightening as she got closer and closer to climax. Their pants and moans were drowned out by the raging rainstorm outside. All that mattered was the two of them. Stephanie screamed when she peaked and Dominic's grunt of pleasure soon followed. He collapsed before rolling over, taking her with him.

They both breathed hard as he pushed her hair back from her face. So many emotions floated through her mind but the main one was contentment, of finally finding her new home in the world. Resting her hand on his chest, she snuggled in closer. He stroked her hair and dropped those sweet, light kisses to her temple that she craved so much. A rumble of thunder sounded in the distance, later followed by a brief flash of light. It was as if they were the only two people in the world and the cabin was their oasis.

"I think the storm has passed." Dominic's voice was raspy and deep.

"What storm?" Stephanie rose on her elbow and touched her fingers to his chin. "I didn't hear a thing." He cured her of those nightmares from so long ago and gave her sweet dreams she would always remember.

Chapter Twenty-Two

Dominic

It was the first time he'd ever woken up next to a woman. Even years ago, when he and Angelia dated, they'd never spent the night together. She'd come from a very overprotective family. He'd tried to be the nice guy. Before every date, he'd shown up with flowers. Little good that did. The last time he bought flowers was to lay them at her grave.

Kissing the head of the woman next to him, he erased those thoughts from his mind. From now on the past was dead and buried, just like all those he'd killed, either directly or indirectly. Stephanie snuggled closer and his heart threatened to jump from his chest. She'd agreed to be his. At least he hoped so and that it wasn't just the heat of the moment. Either way, he was keeping her. He may sound like a kid who brought a stray cat home and was declaring it to his parents but it was true. The woman by his side was where she belonged, now and forever.

"Good morning." Stephanie peeked up at him through a curtain of soft blonde hair. Her green eyes had never been more beautiful. Even her cheeks were a pretty pink. Her fingers weaved their way across his chest before resting below the whiskers of his beard. He noticed very quickly that she loved to touch the hair on his head and his chin.

"Morning." Not very romantic words for how he was feeling right now. All he could do was stare at the most beautiful woman he'd ever seen. He hugged her closer, as if she might disappear into thin air.

"Morning." She blushed and nuzzled his neck.

"Hungry?" He sure had worked up an appetite.

"Only for you."

He kissed her again and she laid her head on his chest. Her long strands of gold hair spread across his chest. He felt like a king. He had everything a man could want in the world. The phone on the bedside table buzzed and reality hit him in the gut. Today was the day.

A quick glance at the screen told him exactly what he knew it would be. It was a text from Jasper, short and sweet.

The results are in. Roman's office, 10:00 a.m., and bring the girl.

The girl? When did she become "the girl" and not Stephanie? Did they find out the same story she'd shared with him last night? Or would he be finding out a different story?

"What is it?" She rose on her elbow and flipped

her hair over her bare shoulder. His eyes automatically narrowed in on her full breasts. A man would have to be dead below the waist not to.

"It's nothing." Dom looked away. His stomach was in knots.

"It's something." Her hand forced his gaze back to hers. "What's wrong?"

"I've got to go to a meeting at Roman's. It's at ten and you're coming with me." He sat up, tossed the sheets aside, and put his feet on the floor, but she wasn't letting him go. Her arms wrapped around his waist as she rested her head against his back.

"Is this the end?"

Dominic patted her hand and turned her way. "He just wants to talk. Let's get dressed and get it over with." The last thing he wanted to do was look her in the eyes. For years, emotions were something others had, but right now fear was all over his face. He couldn't lose her. Not now, not ever.

Stephanie quietly dressed. She must have sensed something was up but didn't ask any questions. Not bothering to make breakfast, they stopped at the Genoa Java Shop. They both deserved the good stuff to prep for what might come later.

The drive through town was uneventful. It was peak tourist season but most were either in the shops or out on their boats. In no time at all, they were waved through the gate at the Caponelli compound. He parked his truck in the shade and walked around to open the door for Stephanie. It was the first time he'd noticed how she dressed. In a black skirt and ivory blouse, she looked like she was going for a job interview or was on trial. Her wavy hair was pulled back into a ponytail. Both hands held her coffee cup tightly as she took a sip.

"Don't worry. Everything will be fine." He pressed a hand to her lower back and guided her toward the front door.

Arlo opened it before they even started up the steps. "Dominic. Stephanie. Roman is waiting for you in his office." He gave no inclination of what was to come.

"Is Madison here?" Stephanie stopped in front of the man.

"No, the seamstress called in sick so she had to go into work. Jasper is with her."

As soon as they stepped inside, Stephanie took hold of his elbow. "That's not good. Because of me, she had to go to the store. Roman will be pissed."

"It's her business. If she didn't want to run it, she should sell it."

"But I work there." She frowned. "At least I used to."

Her future was unknown and they both knew it.

The doors to Roman's office were wide open. He sat at his large desk. His focus was divided between the papers in his hand and the computer. When he saw them approach, Roman dropped the papers and stood up. It was morning and he was already dressed in a three-piece suit and tie.

"Thanks for coming." He motioned for them to take a seat in the two chairs in front of the desk and Arlo closed the door behind them.

Roman sat back in his desk chair and Arlo sat to the side.

"First of all, I don't like secrets." He rested his elbows on the desk and addressed Stephanie. "I like to know who I'm dealing with so I know what to expect. Anticipation and knowledge are the keys to staying ahead in the business and to staying alive. Wouldn't you agree, Miss Barclay?"

Dominic turned to Stephanie. She wiggled in her seat and peeked his way before turning her attention back to his boss.

"That sounds reasonable."

"And yet you've not been forthcoming with us, have you?"

Most men would have been timid under the gaze of the notorious mob boss, yet Stephanie seemed to sit a little taller. "Sometimes you keep things secret to protect the people you care about."

"And would that include my wife?" His eyebrow lifted as he leaned back and crossed his legs.

"Yes, and everyone in this room."

Roman reached for the file on his desk and flipped through the papers inside. "We ran your prints."

"What?" Stephanie stood up. "How? When?" Her fists were at her hips. "You had no right."

Roman rose and towered over her, even from the other side of the desk. "I have every right to protect my family."

"Easy." Dominic reached for her hand and asked her to sit. She did and Roman followed suit.

"Like I said—" Roman started before he was interrupted again.

"How did you get my prints? Was it Madison?" Her eyes teared as Roman nodded in Dom's direction. Stephanie sighed and looked at the ceiling. "How could you?"

"You wouldn't tell us anything. I wanted to protect you. I will protect you."

"So you know who she is?" This time it was Dominic whom Roman addressed the question to.

"Yes, she's the daughter of a mob boss. She's just like us. Her father wanted her to marry a monster. A man who deals in trafficking women. You don't approve of that any more than I do. I know you don't." Dominic pleaded her case.

"If only it was that easy." Roman grabbed the file again. "Are you going to tell him, or am I?"

Stephanie crossed her arms in front of her chest and reached to twirl her hair but it was up in a ponytail.

The office doors flew open. It was Madison. "What the hell is going on here?" She walked to Stephanie's side. "Are you all right?" A sheepish Jasper followed her in. It was pretty obvious where she found out about the meeting.

"There's nothing to worry about." Roman brushed it off.

"Nothing? You have one of my employees and best friends here in your office and don't bother to tell me?"

"Former employees," Roman corrected.

Madison crossed her arms and glared at her husband.

Roman took a deep breath. "Jasper, close the doors."

He did as told and went to stand by Arlo.

"Madison, please take a seat. We were just about

to go over the result of Stephanie's fingerprint analysis."

She finally took a seat next to the two men. "Analysis? You did this to one of my employees without telling me?"

"An employee that you have been illegally paying all these years," Roman snapped.

Madison crossed her legs, her foot swinging back and forth.

"Is this what this is all about?" Stephanie asked. "I would have just quit if you needed me to."

"I can no longer pay you in cash. We could be audited. We'll get it straightened out." Madison rose and came over to lay a comforting hand on her friend's arm. "You just have to get me a social security number and everything will be fine. Won't it, Roman?" She returned to her seat.

"So back to where we were," Roman started again. "We ran your prints and came up with a very interesting result. You are not and never were Stephanie Barclay. The fingerprints belong to Anastasia 'Stassi' Bravikova. Only heir to one of the biggest Russian crime families on the West Coast."

"What?" Madison gasped. "That can't be true."

Stephanie didn't look her in the eyes but nodded.

"I don't understand. You gave me crap from the beginning about getting involved with Roman and all along you have a background just as shady?"

"Because I know what they are capable of. I was running for my life." She filled them in on what happened and why she'd kept her identity secret for so long. "There's nothing left but for me to go to the police and tell them what happened."

"No," everyone in the room said at once.

"We take care of our own," Roman added.

"But I'm not part of this family." Stephanie frowned and Dominic reached for her hand.

"As Dominic's woman and my wife's friend, you are."

Madison's mouth dropped open as she turned her attention to the two of them. Slowly, she grinned like a cat and sat back in her chair.

"So what do we do?" Dominic wanted the matter dealt with and to get out of there as soon as possible. He just wanted to take her back home. He'd never heard of the Bravikovas before so it meant nothing to him. The name Stassi fit, but would she still want to be called Stephanie? That was all he'd ever known her as.

"We put out some feelers. See if Maksim is still in business. Is Stassi's father part of it?" He shrugged while pushing buttons on his computer. "I have my doubts about it since her escape, though hard, seemed too easy. Also, Al Handy is still alive."

"Thank god." Stephanie smiled for the first time since they'd arrived.

Arlo's phone rang and he answered it. "Who's with him?" Arlo turned to Roman and handed him the phone.

"It's the guards," Arlo told them.

"Send them to the house." Roman ended the call and handed the phone back.

"What's going on? Who's here?" Madison asked.

"Ivan Bravikova and Maksim Kozlov."

Dominic jumped to his feet and pulled a gun from behind his back. She didn't know he had one but it made sense if he was wearing a long-sleeved shirt over a tee on such a hot day. Arlo and Jasper grabbed him before he could run out of the room. There was no doubt in her mind that he would kill Maksim and her father after what she'd told him.

"Sit down." Roman came around the desk and stood in front of the door. "That's an order."

"How did they know I was here?" Stephanie stood, eyes wide. Madison put her arm around her shoulder. The room spun with the thought of having her go back with those men. "Please don't make me go. I'll die first."

"Like Roman said, settle down. We need to find out why they're here." Madison was the voice of reason.

"No one is dying," Roman announced. "At least no one in this room is." He took the gun from Dominic's hand and handed it to Arlo. "Maddy, please take Steph to our bedroom and wait. Jasp and Arlo, bring our guests in here."

"What about me?" Dominic tightened his fists.

"If I can trust you to remain calm, you will stay in here with me. I have a feeling this is going to involve you just as much as the girl. Take a seat over there." Roman pointed at a chair behind the desk. "I want to hear what they have to say."

"I'll do my best, but if I don't like what I hear, you might have to shoot to keep me from ripping their heads off." Dominic turned his attention to Stephanie. "Don't worry, everything will be just fine." He kissed her forehead but it wasn't enough. Stephanie stood on tiptoes and drew him in for a kiss. Everyone in the room would now know she was his and he was hers. And nothing and no one was going to pull them apart.

Chapter Twenty-Three

It was a good thing the chair was iron or he'd probably pull the arms off. His death grip on the chair was the only reason Dom didn't rush across the room to rip the faces off the men sitting across the desk from Roman.

"Gentlemen, to what do we owe the honor of this visit?" Roman played the perfect host and offered them a drink, which both declined.

"We are here for his daughter and my fiancée." The man named Maksim spoke first. "Her name is Anastasia Bravikova."

"We have no one by that name here." His guests didn't want a drink but Roman motioned to Jasper to get him one.

"She goes by the name Stephanie Barclay. We know she's here because we saw this photo of her and your man here." Maksim nodded in Dom's direction, pulled a photo from his pocket, and tossed it on the desk. Roman picked it up and handed it to Dominic. It was the photo taken after the fire. They'd tracked them here. The photo had gone more viral than they first thought.

"She was employed by my wife and is under the protection of this family."

Stephanie's father seemed withdrawn and not happy about finding his long-lost daughter. The smirk on the younger man's face whenever he looked Dom's direction made his blood boil. The jackass knew they were a couple. It was obvious from the photo.

"We made inquiries in town and were told we might find her here. You have no idea how much I've missed my daughter." Mr. Bravikova wiped a tear from his eye and Dom rolled his eyes.

"Yet you failed to search very hard for her," Roman said what Dom was thinking.

"She was distressed." Her father shrugged. "I figured she'd just run off to clear her head. I knew she would come to her senses sooner or later. It just took longer than I thought."

"Clear her head? You said you had people looking for her." Maksim was clearly pissed. "Are you telling me you just let her run off? That you hadn't been looking all this time when you said you were." He grabbed Ivan by his lapels.

"Of course I didn't let her run off. You know she's not allowed to be without a guard. I searched everywhere for her." He shook the younger man's hand away. "I'm just stating the fact that she was unhappy about the arrangement. Who's to say a little time away wouldn't help her to see it was the right thing to do?"

Maksim's face reddened. The guy looked like a fool. He had a future bride who would rather go into hiding than be trapped with him. "I want to see my fiancée now." Maksim leaned forward. "If I have to wait any longer, I will tear this place apart piece by piece. Do you understand me?" He rose.

Roman laughed and leaned back in his chair. "You are a guest in my house for the moment, but the minutes till you are thrown out are ticking. Now sit the fuck down."

Maksim narrowed his eyes but did as told.

"She's contracted. I've heard of you and your wife. You know what that means just as much as I do." Maksim beat his chest. "Stassi is mine."

"Contracts can be broken," Dominic piped up.

Roman didn't say anything but his body language said it all. He was not to get involved and his boss wanted to kill Maksim just as much as he did, but this was business.

"This one has consequences. You see," Maksim leaned forward and pointed to the man next to him, "Daddy here didn't manage his finances too well. Our family has been keeping him afloat ever since the deal was signed. Now it is time to pay up."

"Maksim! That's not the truth and you know it. I thought it was a good match." Ivan's face was red as he focused on the carpet. "At least I used to."

Maksim scoffed and folded his arms across his chest. "We have come to collect Stassi and leave."

"That's not going to happen," Roman responded. Dominic knew that his boss didn't like Stephanie and yet he was defending her on his behalf.

"Like I said, we have a signed contract and that cannot be broken. Ivan will lose all honor and respect with the West Coast families. He will be finished."

Mr. Bravikova hung his head. Dom didn't know if he should hate him or feel sorry for him.

"What if we bought the contract?" Roman asked.

Dominic inched forward in his seat. Whatever it took, he would find the money to buy it.

"It's not for sale." Maksim wasn't budging. "We don't need the money."

"You obviously need something or you wouldn't be here." Roman stood up and rounded the desk. "I'm thinking that, at one time, Mr. Bravikova had something you needed and he thought he could benefit from the match also. I think the contract may have started out innocent enough but then something happened. Maybe Stephanie, or Stassi, whatever you wish to call her, found out what a monster you were and decided to get out of town before you prevented her from telling anyone about it." Both men were silent and looked everywhere but at Roman. "And maybe Ivan here changed his mind and didn't want his little girl mixed up in this either but it was too late. He didn't want to get mixed up in your dirty business. Maybe left the cage door open so the little bird could get away."

"I knew you had to have a hand in that. You will pay, and so will Stassi, every single night as I—" Maksim's words were lost as Dominic rushed the man and punched him in the face. Arlo and Jasper jumped in to keep him from killing him. Chairs were flipped over and papers fluttered from Roman's desk.

"Stop!" Roman shouted as they pulled Dom to the side and Maksim slowly got off the floor. Blood streamed from his nose and he wiped it away with the back of his hand.

"I see you are not going to cooperate as I hoped. So I will make you a deal." Maksim had everyone's attention as he stood and placed a hand on Ivan's shoulder. "You can't buy the contact but you can win it. Are you a gambling man, Caponelli?"

"I'm listening." Roman leaned against his desk. It killed Dominic to remain quiet as they talked about Stephanie's future as if she were a horse they were trading.

"You have to fight for her. A fight to the death." He pointed around the room. "Any takers?"

"I'll fight for her." Dominic shook off the hands of those holding him but they remained by his side.

"I thought you would." Maksim had a sick smile on his face. "You survive, you keep the girl. You die, I get Stassi, Bravikova's shipping contracts, and a piece of the action here."

Dom's heart sank. There was no way Roman would risk a part of his business. The business his father had spent years building. Yet Roman walked over and stood in front of him.

"Are you sure? This is to the death. Are you willing to die for her?"

"Yes. Anything to keep her from this monster," Dominic declared, and then even Ivan agreed to the terms.

"Remember, you have to survive," Maksim reminded him. "You die and she's mine to do whatever I want with. Maybe I will have her rejoin her friends. If they're still alive."

"I will win and then I'll kill you," Dominic

promised.

"Oh, no." He waved his finger. "That's not part of the deal. If by some lucky chance you do win, I want the promise that I will not be harmed." He turned his head toward Roman.

"On my word, no member of the Caponelli family will harm you." Roman placed his hand over his heart.

"Good, then we have a deal." Maksim stood and shook hands with Roman. "Tomorrow night, then. I'm anxious to take my bride and go home." He threw a card on the desk. "You name the location and we'll be there."

"We have a spot. I'll make sure it's clear."

"Good, and one last thing. No one touches my fiancée or the deal's off, especially you." He pointed at Dominic and Roman nodded. Maksim straightened his tie and left. Ivan trailed behind somberly.

"Jasper, make sure you see them off the property." Roman sighed and returned to his desk.

"Yes, sir." He left the room as Arlo picked up chairs and the papers littering the floor.

"I won't let you down. I won't let Stephanie down." Never had he feared a fight but this had too much riding on it.

"Go do what you have to do to get ready. Whoever he has lined up will be tough. It won't be Maksim in the ring."

"What?" That would have been icing on the cake to punch the punk's head into the ground.

"Maksim's a coward. He'll find someone good, don't doubt it. I have no doubts you will win.

212

You've done it many times, but this is different. Don't lose focus."

"I won't. But if I do, believe me, I will come back from hell to take him home with me."

"I'd expect nothing less. Do us proud. I know you will."

"Thanks." Dominic nodded.

Stephanie burst into the office, followed by Maddy. "We just saw them leave. What happened?"

"He wouldn't sell the contract so we made a different deal." Roman kissed his wife's cheek.

"What kind of deal?" Stephanie wandered to Dominic's side and Madison sat on her husband's desk.

"I'm fighting for you," Dom said.

"I know you are, but what happened?" She glanced around, but everyone was avoiding her gaze. "What is it?"

Dominic put both hands on her shoulders. "I'm fighting for you. A match to the death. You go with the winner."

"What?" She shook her head and stepped back.

"It's the only way."

"No, you can't do that. No. No. No. I couldn't live with it if you died." Her hand reached to twirl her hair and he took it in his.

"Don't worry. I've never lost a match."

"Match? This is to the death. I won't let you."

"It's done." He hugged her to his chest. "Just understand that I will win."

"When is it?" Her voice was muffled by his shirt.

"Tomorrow night."

Her sob hurt more than any knife ever had.

"I need you to do something for me. I have to get ready for this. As much as I want to spend the night with you, I can't be distracted. It's also part of the deal, I'm not even supposed to touch you. You have to stay here with Madison. Can you do that for me?" When he pulled her from his embrace, tears ran down her face. "Don't cry. Okay?"

She bit her lip. "I can't not cry. I have to be there."

"No." The last thing he needed was for her to see him kill or be killed.

"Yes. You are risking your life for me. I deserve to be there."

"It's not safe," Dominic tried.

"Stassi will stay by my side," Roman stated, and all eyes turned. He'd called her Stassi instead of Stephanie. "She is the daughter of Ivan Bravikova. We must respect her wishes."

"Then I will be there also." Madison stood. From the look on her face, she wasn't taking no for an answer.

"This isn't some MMA match on TV. Someone will die and it won't be pretty. I don't want you to see me like that." The last thing he wanted was for Stephanie to watch him die trying to save her. It would haunt her forever, just as Angelia's death had haunted him. It would be easier to just take Maksim out and kill him, but there was a code in the mafia. Honor and respect were everything. Someone would show up to avenge his death even if the man deserved it. This had to be done the right way or there would be consequences.

"I will be there to cheer you on and to celebrate

214

your win." Stephanie wiped the tears from her eyes.
She wasn't taking no for an answer either.

Chapter Twenty-Four

Stephanie

Her stomach had been in knots ever since she heard about the fight.

"You need to eat." Madison hovered like a mother hen.

"There's no way I could eat anything." Stephanie typed as fast as she could on the keyboard. Somehow, her laptop had showed up and her story just got another twist. Never had she expected this turn of events and it helped to get her emotions down before she forgot. Tomorrow, if things didn't go well, she'd be forced to leave. Go back to living a nightmare that she would never wake from. Would living even matter if Dominic was dead? Her life would be over also. She'd be empty, a ship adrift in a crazy sea.

No matter what, if Dominic was killed, she would not rest until Maksim was dead. Stephanie would pretend to be the dutiful mob wife and then when he least expected it, she'd drive a stake through his cold, evil heart.

"Then how about a protein shake or something?" Maddy's voice brought her back to the present. "You have to be strong for Dominic. I'll go make one and I'm not leaving until you drink it." Frustrated, she left, only to soon be replaced by Roman.

He knocked on the open door. The man seemed to have changed his tune since finding out about her background, or was it because of Dom? He certainly couldn't be happy about the change in events. "Can I have a word?"

She kept typing but nodded to the vacant chair by her side. He was silent until she shut the laptop and sat back in her chair. "What?"

"How are you doing?" What the hell? He was concerned about her? Where was this guy when he talked about having her killed just a few days ago?

"How am I doing? How do you think I am doing? My god. Dominic is out there somewhere doing who knows what to get ready for this fight." Stephanie broke down. "I can't lose him."

Roman took her hand but she pulled it away. "You won't lose him."

"Can you promise that? Make it come true?" She was angry at both men. How dare they gamble with her life and theirs.

"Did he ever tell you how we met?"

"No." She shook her head and some of her hair came loose from the knot she'd haphazardly put it up in. "Just that you saved him. From what I haven't a clue."

"I'll tell you, then. I was in Italy when I heard

217

the story of Dominic. He was a legend in the underworld there. A fighter. When I dug a little deeper, I found out why he was so successful."

Stephanie wiped the hair away from her face and listened. "Go on."

"Dominic was just an ordinary guy who worked out at a local gym, but everyone knew he had talent. Dom could have been very successful as a fighter. He knew boxing, karate, every kind of mixed martial arts you can think of. So why would a man like that end up in an illegal fighting ring?"

"I don't know. Money?" She'd seen him spar in the gym but couldn't picture him in some fight club.

"It wasn't just any fighting ring. Many of the main events were to the death. No amount of money is worth dying for."

"And yet many people do." It was a somber thought.

"Like I said, he was a normal guy and one who could have been very successful. Yet he fought, won, and killed for years," Roman continued.

"Years?" Steph still couldn't picture him covered in his opponent's blood, but tomorrow she'd see it firsthand.

"Yes." Roman patted her shoulder.

"So why did he do it?"

"The girl he loved had been taken by the same ones who organized the fights. If Dominic didn't do what they said, they threatened she'd be raped and then murdered. He sold his soul to save hers."

"So you rescued him and she was spared?" The thought of him with another woman was unsettling, but everyone had a past.

"I could only save one, but I knew a man with that much loyalty and heart would be an asset. I also won't tolerate anyone that harms women. We rescued him out of that hell hole where they held them. He didn't want to go at first. Dom was worried about what would happen to her, but by then it was too late."

"What happened to her? Where is she?"

"She was taken, the same time as he. Sold into some sex trade in Eastern Europe. When we finally tracked her down, it was too late. She'd slit her wrists with a razor blade. They tossed her in a ditch out in a field. The bastards. We made sure she was given a decent burial in her hometown."

"Oh no." She couldn't help but feel pain for the both of them.

"We got him cleaned up and brought him to the States. It took a long time for him to get over everything. The loss. The never-ending fights. The death."

"I can't imagine. I'm so sorry for what happened to them both." It brought back the horror of what had happened to her friends. Maksim would pay for this. She'd make sure of it.

"That's one of the reasons he doesn't like crowds and closed in places."

"Then I can't let him do that again. It would destroy him. I can't be responsible for destroying Dominic."

"It'd destroy him if you went with Maksim, especially after knowing what kind of monster he is and what he's done. Dom never wanted to fall in love again after what happened but he did. He loves

219

you. Anyone can see that. As they say, love conquers all. Believe in him. Believe in the both of you." Roman got to his feet. "I do." He left the room just moments before Madison returned with a protein drink in one hand and a wine glass in the other. She placed the shake beside Stephanie and then took a seat on the Davenport.

"I have no clue what's in it but it's one of the protein things that the guys buy in a huge jug. It's supposed to be good for you so drink up."

Stephanie took a sip. It was thick and milky but it filled her belly.

"I saw Roman leaving." Madison kicked her shoes off and spread out on the couch. "Did he tell you about Dominic?"

"You knew and didn't tell me?" It hurt to be the only one who didn't know of his past but she could see why. The scars that man had to deal with were many.

"It wasn't my story to tell." She sighed. "I thought it better for Dom to do it. Roman asked me if you knew and I said I didn't think so. He must have decided it was the right time to tell you."

"I'm so confused right now, not to mention being scared to death."

"That's understandable." Maddy swung her feet back to the floor and took a sip of her wine.

"I have to see Dominic and tell him how I feel."

"Not now. He's with Jasper. They have to get things ready and are negotiating terms of the fight."

"Terms?" Maddy and she should be talking about dresses and weddings or other things involving work, not rules and negotiations for a fight. "It's to the death. What else is there to talk about?"

Madison frowned. "Do you really want to know?"

"Yes. I do. I have to be brave for him tomorrow. I don't want to do anything that will distract him or add any more stress to the situation."

"They are still talking about locations, weapons, seconds."

"Wait, what?" She placed her chin in her palm and fought the urge to cry. "I know I grew up in a crime family but I know nothing of these fights."

"Basically, it has rules and no rules." Madison really had become the mob boss wife. Drinking wine and talking about a duel like it was a country club event. It was all too much. If only she could just fall asleep and have this be a dream.

"The location has to be approved by both. No one wants to walk into an ambush made to look like an accident. From what I understand, there will be no weapons for the first five minutes. After that they can grab anything that is around—there will be weapons, except for guns, on the floor to use. As for seconds, if one of the main fighters doesn't show up, their second will take their place."

Stephanie held the cool drink to her forehead. "I think I'm going to be sick."

"Do you want me to get the doctor?" Her friend set her glass on a table and reached for her phone.

"No, there is no cure for this." That's why she had to write her story down. No one would believe this, and if she did end up leaving with Maksim, Stephanie wanted everyone to know about the hero who gave his life for hers. But she couldn't think like that. Dominic was going to win. "I know Dom will be there, but who is his second?"

"Jasper."

That made sense.

"And Maksim? Who is his?"

"From what I understand, Maksim is the second."

"What? That can't be. He's the one who suggested it, from what I understand."

"He was, but everyone knows Dom would kick his ass. We don't know the man yet but it's a good bet it will be a very tough opponent."

"I can't believe this nightmare." Her head spun.

"After tomorrow, it will all be over. You can start planning for the rest of your lives together," Maddy reassured her. "I'll design your dress."

"What dress?" As much as she tried to be hopeful, the vision of herself in a black dress kneeling by his grave flashed before her eyes.

"Your wedding dress. What did you think I meant?"

She closed her eyes and let out a sob.

"I'm calling the doctor and getting you a sedative."

"No. No drugs. I have to be strong and I will be." Stephanie said a quick prayer, something that she planned on doing a lot in the next twenty-four hours.

***

Dominic

Normally, he'd have weeks of training for a fight, but there wasn't much he could do in this short amount of time. Luckily, he maintained a good regimen of running and working out in the gym. Still, was it going to be enough?

He hit the punching bag that Jasper held in place. This was not how he pictured his life ending and he wasn't ready to go yet.

"That pussy won't even fight." Jasper cut into his thoughts. "Who do you think you will go against?"

"The best prick he can find." Dom kicked the bag and nearly took his friend off his feet. As much as he tried to dislike and distance himself from the guy, he was the first one to step up and be his second. Not that he needed one, there was no way he would miss it.

"Just so you know, no matter what happens, I have your back. Roman won't tell how he's going to take care of Maksim if you lose, which you won't, but you have my word that man will not touch a hair on her head. I will keep her safe. Not because I want her for myself but because she is family and is yours."

Dominic hugged the bag for a moment. There was a lump lodged in his throat. The last few days had been almost too much to handle. Emotions had run high, and his heart had grown almost too large for his chest. Nurtured with love not just for his woman but the family he'd been welcomed into.

Being his second was merely an honorary title,

but Jasper meant it. Maksim took that spot for his fighter but there was no way he would bloody his face. The man was a coward, and the jury was still out on her father. Whoever he hired to fight would be there, no questions asked.

"Come on. Let's do some sparing." Jasper broke the tension. "Just don't hit my face. The chicks love me."

"That so?" Dominic smiled for the first time in hours. "Then I should give you a black eye, might improve your chances."

"Nah, they love me just the way I am." Jasper grabbed some gear and entered the ring. "You got this, dude. I know you do."

"I know I do too." No matter who it was he was fighting, Dom planned on winning. Losing wasn't an option. His life and Stephanie's depended on it.

Chapter Twenty-Five

Stephanie

The whole day moved in slow motion and yet the time of the fight had come too quickly. After finally agreeing to the sleep aid the doctor gave her, Stephanie fell into a fitful slumber. Her nervous stomach still couldn't handle much food but Madison managed to get her to eat some soup and bread sent over from Firenza.

Dominic had sent her flowers. A beautiful bouquet of sunflowers tied with a red ribbon. There was no message but she looked up the meaning of the flower. They stood for loyalty, longevity, and adoration.

Arlo came to collect them at six that evening and take them to the fight. Maddy may have appeared calm on the outside but Stephanie knew she was just as distressed by it as she was. Roman was already there making sure everything was on the up and up.

It was a warm evening yet goosebumps dotted

her arms. Madison was silent as they drove through the town. Tourists walked the street, oblivious to what was about to happen.

"Where are we going?" She couldn't take any more of the unknown.

"It's a garage we sometimes use with the Tribe." Arlo glanced at her in the rearview mirror.

The man probably knew she'd been there with Dom. Everyone always seemed to know what was going on and who was where. "Is Dominic there?"

"Not yet. The fighters will arrive last."

"I know this is crazy and the last thing either of us ever thought we would be a part of when I first ran into Roman at the coffee shop so long ago, but it is our lives now. Show no fear and no tears," Madison advised. The last thing Stephanie wanted to hear was a pep talk but it was exactly what she needed.

"I'll be fine. It will be fine." And she said another prayer for the one she loved. It seemed odd to pray for the death of another but she was. Sometimes you didn't have a choice in picking battles. This was self-defense as far as she was concerned. Payback for all the lives Maksim had stolen. Dominic had to win. He'd fought before to keep a loved one safe and he was doing it again. The man was a hero.

Several black SUVs and a few motorcycles crowded the parking lot. The Mayhem Tribe was the so-called referee of the event. Sure, they were more on board with the Caponellis, but on such short notice, they didn't have much choice.

Arlo parked and helped the women from the

vehicle. Madison was dressed like the queen she was. Designer shoes and an elegant dark blue sheath dress. Stephanie wore a long, flowy, mustard-colored dress and a pair of sandals. It was something she knew Dom would like. They walked in silence to the building and it was quiet in there as well. Flipping her sunglasses on top of her head, Stephanie stepped into the shade of the building.

Arlo guided them to their seat. The women sat on two folding chairs while the men circled the border of the room. A couple bikers pointed her way, and she startled. They were there that night back in California. A bead of sweat ran down her chest and between her breasts. They smiled and she calmed the urge to puke. It made sense that they would still be keeping company with Maksim. That man made her skin crawl. Just thinking about her life if she had stayed and married him caused her to teeter in the chair.

"They'll be arriving soon." Arlo handed each of them a bottle of water. She'd need something stronger to get through the rest of the day. Her stomach was in knots. The whole thing was just crazy and she refused to even look in the monsters' direction again.

"I thought only Mayhem members were to be here," Madison said.

"I guess Maksim wanted some backup just in case. They just arrived. You'd think he'd have soldiers here but we're starting to think members of his own family might not even know all he is involved in," Arlo replied.

"You both don't need to be here." Roman

showed up dressed like it was a day at the office and stopped in front of the ladies. At least he had shed the suit coat in the heat but still wore a dress shirt and tie. "I can make excuses if you want to leave."

"No, I have to be here for Dominic. No matter what happens, I am here for him." Her voice shook and so did her hands.

"It will start soon." He nodded and then stood behind his wife.

A biker with a Mayhem cut strolled to the center of the room. "For those who don't know me, I'm Forge, president of the Tribe of Mayhem. The fight will begin as soon as the fighters arrive."

"I think they're here," a young man with a prospect patch announced from the open door. The crowd hushed and the sound of car doors shutting sounded from outside.

Dominic walked in first, followed by Jasper. They couldn't have stopped her if they wanted to. She ran to him and hugged him tightly. His strong arms engulfed her. He kissed the top of her head and then framed her face. His lips touched hers in a kiss that would have to last a lifetime. It spoke of their past, their present, and hopefully their future. She clung to him until Arlo gently drew her away and guided her back to her seat. It was as if one of her books had come to life. The whole thing felt like a dream but it was real and happening right in front of her. Madison put her arm around her as Dominic and Jasper walked to the middle of the room.

Not until now did she notice he was barefoot and

only wearing shorts. His long hair tightly braided and pulled back. Jasper stood behind him dressed in sweatpants and a tee. They both nodded to Forge.

Soon, another vehicle could be heard on the crushed rock parking lot. Anyone traveling by would have to wonder what was going on but they'd set up roadblocks on the seldom traveled side road. Doors slammed again and everyone in the room stretched their necks to see who the other competitor would be.

The prospect by the door looked up and took a step back. Her heart sank when she saw how big the guy was. He was huge. The man was dressed just like Dom. Barefoot, bare chest, and wearing shorts. As he neared, she could see he had even more scars than Dominic. This man was used to fighting as well.

When he neared the center of the room, the man stood a head taller than pretty much everyone. He was followed by Maksim, who wore a smirk on his face. The guy already thought he'd won. They both greeted Forge and stood in the circle in the middle of the room.

"Dominic," the other fighter addressed him, "you're smaller than I remember."

"And you're older," Dominic remarked with a snarl, and then he said something only Jasper could hear. He nodded and glanced at Roman.

"Both are here, so let's get this started. You are?" Forge asked the new fighter.

"Oscar," the giant man stated.

Forge held the wrist of each fighter in his hand like he was at an official match. "The rules are, there are no rules. The first five minutes you can only use your body. Hits, kicks, knees are all fine. After I call time, you can use any of the weapons lying on the floor, but only those weapons."

Stephanie's vision blurred as she noticed the different tools lying around the floor. She'd ignored them at first as they were simple tools found in any garage. Items like hammers, chains, screwdrivers, a saw. *A saw!* She moaned.

"No guns are allowed." Forge directed his comment to Maksim. "If we see anyone trying to hand one of the fighters a gun, or any other kind of weapon, you will be tossed out. Do both fighters agree to the terms?"

Both men said yes. Forge and the two men's seconds stepped back.

Jasper traveled to Roman's side and Maksim joined his group of bikers.

Forge had one of those old-time railroad watches attached to a chain. He checked the time and yelled, "The five minutes starts now."

Both fighters held their hands out, making jabs to test the other. Dom took a hit to the jaw but it just nicked him. If it had been a direct hit, he'd probably have gone to the ground. Dom kicked his opponent in the chest. A normal man would have fallen backward, but this guy remained strong. The jabs and hits continued for a minute until Oscar rushed Dom and threw him to the floor. The sound of bone and skin hitting the cement caused everyone to cringe.

Stephanie bit her finger to keep from calling out. Her love had just missed landing on a rusty crowbar by inches. The last thing she wanted to do was distract him. The fighters battled it out on the floor, rolling around. Wrestling exerted more strength than being on your feet boxing. Dominic struggled to get on top and finally got Oscar in a chokehold. Oscar threw his head back and his skull connected with Dom's nose. Blood ran from his nostrils and he lost his grip. Oscar flipped Dom over and they were a sweaty mixture of limbs for the next several minutes as they grappled to gain the upper hand.

Her heart raced a hundred miles an hour as she watched. It was horrible to witness yet she couldn't look away. At any second, his life could be snuffed out like a candle. They were both bruised and bloody by the fourth minute. It felt like forty minutes to her. She wobbled in her seat. Jasper now stood by her side and kept a tight hold on her shoulder. If she passed out, he would catch her. It was a given that he was there to look after her at the command of Dom. He hadn't looked her way since it started. There was no way he would be able to.

Oscar was a very fierce competitor but Dom was fast on his feet. Three times they ended up on the floor. Then they were back on their feet, punching with everything they had. Oscar took a punch to the gut that had him wincing. The more they sweat, the more slippery they were to hang onto.

Out of the corner of her eye, she saw that Roman's hands were on his wife's shoulders. Madison was as distressed as she was.

"Who is this man?" Roman asked Jasper.

"He's the man who trained Dom back in Italy." Jasper spoke so only they could hear.

"Before or after he was captured?" she wondered.

"Both."

Forge stepped near the men grunting and groaning again on the floor. "Five minutes are up. Choose your weapons." The surrounding men kicked the tools bordering the ring closer to the center. Dom had Oscar in another good hold and swung him around. The man's leg ended up in the barbwire. The barbs punctured his skin and blood spattered the floor.

Oscar slipped from the hold and grabbed a nearby bat. He wheeled it back and swung it straight at Dominic's head.

Chapter Twenty-Six

Dominic

They say your life flashes before your eyes right before you die. Nothing flashed, but when he witnessed the horror in Stephanie's gaze, he knew it was time to move. The breeze from the swing of the bat cooled his heated flesh. Never did he think he would be back fighting again. That part of his life was a closed door that was never to be opened again, but here he was. Not only that, but he was up against the man who had trained him. Fucking Oscar!

The man had been a friend, a mentor, and then when Dom found out why he'd been so nice to him, the devil. It had all been a plan to get him into that twisted fight club. When he refused, they took Angelia. Now he was fighting for a woman again, only this time he would win. But it wasn't going to be easy. Nothing ever was. The brute knew what he was doing. His opponent may have been older but he knew every trick in the book. Knew every delicate pressure point on the body. All the spots that one poke, one jab, or one well-placed kick could knock a person to their knees.

But Dominic had been a good student and he remembered those spots as well, and Oscar was a big target. In no time they were both sweating and breathing hard. It was hot, humid, and emotions were running high. Emotions that sometimes caused mistakes. One of them would die soon. Some of his former battles had gone fast. Inexperienced fighters came out swinging before taking the time to study the weaknesses of those they were up against.

Oscar had a bad knee. It was the opposite of the one he led with. Dom had tried to kick it a few times but missed. The man was still quick on his feet, that was for sure. There were a variety of weapons and tools scattered across the floor but none appealed to him. Dominic preferred to keep his prey close. Objects needed to be swung with force to do the most damage, so keeping a stronghold kept the other from using one effectively.

His body was bruised and battered. The cool concrete floor was littered with dirt that stuck to his skin. The crowd yelled encouragements but it was just static. The main thing was to stay focused. Tune the rest of the world out. That was sometimes hard to do when his life was at stake but he still managed to slow things down at least in his mind.

When Oscar swung the bat, it gave Dom the perfect opportunity to strike the side of his opponent's bleeding leg. Dom kicked it from the side and the man stumbled and went down.

Dominic lunged to get him in a chokehold but his competitor slid from his grasp and ended up flipping Dom to the ground. His fall to the cement caused his teeth to rattle. He groaned as his body told him he'd just aged fifty years.

Nothing was broken and he shook his head to clear the cobwebs. Dom fought the urge to find Stephanie in the crowd and make sure she was okay, there was no time. Jasper had promised to keep her safe and he'd put his trust in him. Right now, he had other things to worry about. Oscar had picked up and started the chainsaw that had been among their weapons of choice. The smell of gas and smoke filled the air and he recognized the cries of the woman he loved in the background.

Oscar came after him while he was still on the ground. Dom grabbed a crowbar to hold the saw at bay as the man above him pushed it closer to his face. Sparks flew and burned parts of his flesh. Dominic took advantage of the awkward stance and the strain the heavy saw was putting on Oscar's back. When the man lifted it briefly, Dominic struck the man's leg with the metal bar. The crack echoed in the room as it shattered his enemy's knee. The saw fell from his hands and skidded across the floor.

With the man on his back, Dominic pounced. He tried to go for Oscar's throat but the guy would not give up. Oscar's arms were the size of Dom's legs. The years had added rings of muscle and strength to this beast just like age did to the rings on a tree. Oscar also had a longer reach. Whereas Dom could not reach his throat, Oscar had his thick fingers around his and he squeezed tight. It would be a minute at most before Dom would lose air and go limp. There was no way that was going to happen. If it took his dying breath, which it might be, Oscar would win.

As the grip on his throat had him seeing stars, Dom caught sight of something lying by the shoulder of the man beneath him. It was an ice pick. The first time he tried to reach it, he caused it to move farther. With just seconds until he passed out, he made one last grasp. That was all he had, one last chance to save Stephanie. Dominic threw his knee into the guy's gut and the grip around his neck loosened.

With the pick held securely in both hands, he plunged it to the hilt into Oscar's heart. The man's eyes bulged. It was over. His lungs would fill with blood in seconds.

"That's for Anastasia." Dom withdrew it and stabbed him again. "That's for Angelia." He repeated the process several more times. "And that is for all the lives you forced me to take to protect her." Foam and blood dripped from Oscar's mouth. Dominic stood and dropped the bloody tool to the floor. The metal clunked on the cement. Everyone was silent except for the final gurgles sounding from the man on the ground.

Dom staggered back. His legs shook as his heart raced with adrenaline. Everyone was quiet and just stared. Blood dripped from his fingers and covered his chest. Finally, he heard Jasper yell, "Fuck yeah!" and the crowd followed suit with shouts and applause. His gaze finally settled on Stephanie. Her face was pale and her eyes were wide. Jasper still stood behind her, his hand resting on her shoulder. Dominic may have won the battle but he'd lost the only thing that mattered. How would she ever get over what he'd done? What he was?

She'd be better off with Jasper. The guy had grown on him. He knew deep down the man had a heart, and once it was taken, that lucky woman would always be first in his life. A few of the biker crew members came up and slapped him on the back but he was still in a daze.

Without a word to anyone, Dom walked out of the building. His skin was cold and clammy with sweat and blood. The warmth from the sun was heaven and he stood with his face toward the sky. He tore his fingers through the braid on his head. One of the first things Oscar did when he arrived was shaved Dom's head, and that's the way it remained the whole time he was held there. It was risky to have hair as a competitor could tear it from your head. A lot of good that did the man lying on the floor.

Dom wandered over toward the wood fence on the edge of the property and stared back at the garage. No one had come out yet. That was a blessing. He wasn't ready to talk to anyone. The white van he used was parked in the lot and would soon be used to cart Oscar to the funeral home. Wiping the back of his hand across his forehead, it finally hit him that it could be him right now taking his last ride in the van. There was no doubt in his mind that he would win, but going against Oscar hadn't been in the plan. That had shocked the hell out of him, but he was glad in the end. That man would've been able to do to anyone else what he'd done to him.

Stephanie was free now. Would she go home to California to be with her father or just go where no one could find her?

"Dom," she called from the building, and then awkwardly ran across the parking lot in her sandals. The woman should be running away from him, not toward him, but she was.

His heart ached as she'd never looked more beautiful. Her pretty dress so fresh and clean, while he was covered in filth. They were total opposites in every way. It had never been clearer than now. He loved her with all his soul but happy endings were only in books. Now she would give him the heave-ho—"Thanks for saving me, but no, thanks."

But she didn't. Stephanie leaped into his arms. Her dress was now stained with blood but she didn't seem to care as she covered his face in kisses. "Are you hurt? Do you need a doctor?"

"No." He shook her off. "You'll ruin your dress."

"I don't give a damn about the dress. You risked your life for me. Fought for me. I can't ever thank you enough." She framed his face with her hands.

"You don't have to thank me and you don't owe me anything."

Stephanie cocked her head like a confused puppy. "What's wrong?"

"Don't you understand?"

"No. I love you."

"Still?" Dominic chuckled and waved his hand

238

toward the shed as they carried Oscar's body to the van. "After seeing that you still want to be with me?"

"It's because of who I am that you had to do that. Do you still want to be with me?" She folded her arms across her chest. "Seems to me we are the perfect ones to be together. Perfectly messed up from perfectly messed up situations. We aren't picket fence type people but you're the one I want. You know where I come from and still stood by me. I know who you are and what you did and I'm still standing here. I'll be standing by you for the rest of my life. Am I wasting my time? Did you change your mind?"

Could it be? Could they really be happy and go on from here? If she was willing to try, he wasn't giving up. Stephanie was the best thing that ever happened in his life, and if he had to fight for her again, he would.

"Well?" Her lower lip trembled and there were tears in her eyes.

Dom took a step forward. "I told you I don't fall in love but it was a lie. It's the only lie I ever told you. The truth is you've been in my heart from the first time I ever saw you. You held the piece to my heart that's been missing for such a long time. I love you and always have. Together, I feel normal." He smiled. "Well, as normal as one could be in this business. If you can stand to be with a scarred, broken fighter, I can handle being with the daughter of a mob boss."

"Try to keep me away." She wrapped her arms around him again and he crushed his lips to hers. It wasn't a tender kiss but one of possession, of need, of passion. They belonged to each other and no one was ever going to tear them apart again.

"Isn't this touching?" Maksim snarled, and clapped his hands.

Chapter Twenty-Seven

Stephanie

She cringed at his voice. How she wished it was he who had just died. "What do you want, Maksim? You lost."

"Let's be reasonable. Your father needs our business or he'll go under." He narrowed his eyes at her. "I'll make sure of that."

"Anybody who gets involved with you deserves it."

"It's time for you to leave," Roman said. She hadn't realized that they were drawing a crowd. Roman, Maddy, Arlo, and her father now surrounded them. Hopefully, her father hadn't heard what he said, but then the jury was still out on his involvement. If he hadn't signed that damn contract, they wouldn't be here right now. She glanced at Dominic. If it weren't for that damn contract, she wouldn't be here at all.

Maksim started to argue about some unfair advantage but Roman shut that down fast. "The

241

battle was won fair and square. You leave now. I have some business to discuss with Ivan and it doesn't include you."

"This isn't fair," the younger man whined.

"This was your idea." Stephanie lunged and kicked him in the nuts. The guy bent over in pain and Dominic held her from behind before she could attack him again. "You are pure evil," she spat. "You deserve to spend eternity in hell for what you did to my friends and all those other girls."

Maksim slowly straightened but ignored her. "You promised me safe passage home, Caponelli, and I'm ready to go."

"Gladly." Roman motioned for one of the SUVs to come over. It stopped and the driver got out and opened the back door. "Take this bastard where he needs to go."

Maksim fumed. His face a bright red and his fists were clenched as he got in.

"Yes, sir." The driver closed the door and then winked at Steph. There was something familiar about the guy. Could it be? Her savior from the past? Briefly, before he got into the front seat, she caught sight of a dog. It was a red-nosed boxer mix, and if she was a betting person, she'd put odds on it that his name was Willy Dawg. A smile crossed her face.

Everyone stared as they drove off.

"He got off easy," Maddy grumbled, and Roman laughed.

"My fierce wife thinks I went easy on him." He placed an arm around her shoulder and kissed her cheek. "Maybe she should run this organization.

The woman is tough as nails."

"He should be in the van with the other guy but I know you promised him no harm." Maddy sometimes forgot she shouldn't speak against her husband in public but he seemed more than a little amused with her comments.

Dominic's work van soon headed off in the same direction.

"I promised him that no one in my family would harm him," Roman clarified.

Maddy stepped toward the road and pointed at the retreating van. "So who was the driver? He wasn't one of our men?"

"That's Jeeper," Ivan said and walked over to his daughter. "He works for me."

"Did you tell him to help me get away?" Stephanie hoped it was true.

"Yes. I did."

***

Stephanie sat with her feet up while she typed on her laptop. This story was taking much longer than she thought as things kept changing. They'd just taken her father to the airport and he was on his way back to the West Coast.

Maksim had joined Oscar in the van heading to the funeral home, so his story was over. After a long talk with Ivan, she discovered that neither he nor Maksim's father knew what he was involved in until she was almost taken that stormy night so long ago. Maksim had used her father's ships to transport women out of the country. He was also

243

blackmailing him from saying anything as he made it look like her father was just as guilty as Maksim was.

The contract had been signed before then. It was his idea to have Jeeper convince her to leave. He'd rather never see her again than have his daughter at the mercy of a madman. They'd had a few days to reunite and he'd talked with Roman about selling the shipping business to some of his contacts out there.

Her father had aged over the years and wished to retire. He'd taken an instant liking to Genoa and was already looking at properties on the lake. Everything was coming together. She hadn't gone back to working at the bridal store. Planning weddings wasn't her passion, writing was. Her book may never sell a million copies, but the fact that she was almost finished with it was a milestone in her life.

She needed to get a job soon, once she received a real Social Security card. Anastasia Bravikova was alive again. There was no need to keep pretending she was someone she wasn't. Everyone still called her Stephanie—that would be too much of a change. Her father had been depositing money into her bank account every month since she'd been gone in the hopes that she might use it if needed. To say she really didn't need to work would be an understatement. She was loaded.

"Almost done." She typed "The End," closed the laptop, and stood.

Dominic walked across the room and kissed her forehead. "I'm so proud of you."

"Thanks. Now to get it published is another thing."

"The fact that you finished it is a huge accomplishment in itself."

"It's a pretty crazy story. That's for sure."

"The true ones usually are." He scooped her up in his arms.

"What are you doing?" Dominic smelled delicious. That fresh, outdoorsy scent that drove her wild. "We have to get to the party." Valentina and Ryan were sharing the news of their pregnancy. It certainly wasn't a secret. The woman glowed and Ryan couldn't be prouder or more overprotective than he was before.

"Let's have a party of our own." He tossed her on their bed and pulled his shirt over his head. She never tired of looking at him. That long hair made her swoon, and when those muscles flexed, her knees went weak.

Stephanie continued to stare as he removed her shirt and bent to kiss her neck. The scruff of his jaw tickled her and she squirmed from his touch. They'd talked a lot in the last week. There were no more secrets between them and Angelia's picture was now in a drawer. That part of his past was over for good. When he slipped her shorts and panties down, there were no more clothes between them either. He was a wonderful lover. Sometimes fierce and overpowering and other times sweet and tender.

They didn't have a lot of time but she didn't need it when the man she was with made her melt on sight. She gasped as his finger dipped between her legs. Stephanie was ready before he even asked.

Her love for this man made her heart want to jump from her chest. Dominic kissed his way from her breasts to her neck to her mouth. He was an electric shock to her system that she'd grown to need on a daily basis just to survive.

Her lids closed when he thrust in. The pace was fast and furious but he never finished before she did. Her man may not use a lot of words but he spoke to her like no one ever could. They rocked back and forth, entwined in every possible way before her world burst and Stephanie floated back to earth. His groan of pleasure echoed in her ears.

Stephanie hugged him tight, tears in the corners of her eyes.

"Are you okay?" Dominic slid his thumb across her cheek. "Did I hurt you?"

"No, never." She smiled. "I'm just happy. I've been lost for so long, wandering alone, but now I have you. I have my father, Madison, Valentina." Stephanie laughed. "Even Roman no longer wants to kill me. Everything is right in the world."

"Yes, it is." He kissed her lips again.

***

Six Months Later

It seemed odd to be at Firenza and not be working the event being held, but this one was for her. The first publisher that she submitted her book to had offered her a contract. It was a dream come true.

Not only that, her whole family, her new family,

were all there to show their support. Valentina looked amazing with her round belly. She wore flats to appease Ryan, who was afraid she would fall in her stilettos. Roman teased Madison about getting to work on producing an heir but so far that hadn't worked. Maddy was scared of babies, never having been around them, but that might change when her sister-in-law had one.

Stephanie had been signing books all night. It wasn't out until Tuesday but she'd received advance copies of *Contract from Hell* from the publisher. Every time she saw the cover, a smile lit up her face. It was of Dominic. You couldn't see his face as it was in the shadows, but it was definitely his hot body. He'd never live down the teasing from the guys but he did it for her. That cover alone would sell books. Lots and lots of books.

Contract from Hell was her story, but to the world, it was a work of fiction. The names had been changed to protect the guilty, the innocent, and the truly awful. She kept her fake name as her pen name.

Stephanie flexed her fingers and looked up. A tall redhead was the next in line for a book. She held out a copy for Stephanie to sign.

"Would you like it personalized?" It was still hard to believe that people actually wanted her autograph. The whole thing was crazy.

"Yes, please. You can make it out to Jackie."

Stephanie signed it and placed a bookmark in the middle. "Thanks so much, and I hope you enjoy the story of Stassi and Diego."

"I'm sure I will. Here's my card. I'm a new

reporter at the *Genoa Globe*, I would love to set up an interview with you." The woman held out a well-manicured hand and placed the card in front of her.

"Okay, that sounds like fun." Publicity was still something she shied away from but it had to be done. "What was your name again?" Stephanie twirled a piece of hair around her index finger.

"Jacqueline Smith," she answered.

"Wow, my favorite angel." Jasper came out of nowhere and stood by her side.

"I'm sorry?" The woman gave him a quick glance from head to toe.

"*Charlie's Angels*. You know, Farrah, Kate, and Jaclyn." He winked. "Jacqueline was my favorite one."

"Yes, well, same name different spelling." She turned her attention back to Steph.

"Both still angels in my eyes." Jasper practically drooled and Stephanie rolled her eyes.

"This is Jasper. Jasper, this is Jackie. She's a reporter at the *Globe*."

"Oh yeah? I have a few stories to tell." Jasper placed a hand on the table. "Let me buy you a drink and I'll tell you a few."

"Maybe next time. Thank you for the book, Miss Barclay. I look forward to reading the story and setting up an interview." Jackie nodded to Jasper and walked off.

"Well, that was rude." Jasper frowned.

"She's a reporter. Probably a good thing you don't tell her any of your stories," Stephanie tried to console him.

"What's up?" Dominic held one of her books in

his hands.

"Jasper struck out with a hot redhead," Stephanie teased.

"She wasn't that hot." Jasper pouted but his eyes kept following the one they talked about around the room. "Maybe I should give her another chance. Make her feel better."

"You do that." Dominic smirked and gave his friend a shove in her direction. Yes, they were friends now. They'd had him over a few times to eat and Stephanie encouraged them to go out for beers now and then when she needed time alone to write. "How's it going?"

"It's amazing. I can't believe all these people showed up for this." She smiled from ear to ear.

"Well, your dad's been telling everyone in town about it. He's very proud of you."

"He's making up for lost time and I'm so glad to have him here." The man stood at the bar talking to Arlo. Arlo was the only one who didn't look happy that night. Rumor was he'd been spending too much time with Layla, Madison's sister, and their father sent him back to Genoa.

"Got enough ink in the pen to sign another one?" Dominic handed his copy of her book across the table.

"Anything for you." She smiled.

"I hope so." Dominic shoved his hands in his pocket and rocked back and forth.

"Uh, okay." Stephanie opened the book he gave her and her heart stopped. It was already signed. By him. In bright red letters. It said, "Will you marry me?"

"Wow." She was stunned.

"I hope that's a yes. I had our names engraved on that wedding sword I made. It'd be a shame to waste it. It's hanging on the wall at home right now." The man wasn't fond of talking yet he was rattling on and on.

Stephanie closed the book, stood up, and walked around to stand in front of him. "That story's over with." Stephanie cupped his jaw with one hand and nodded to the table piled high with books. "But this one is just getting started."

"Is that a yes?" Dominic arched an eyebrow.

"A huge yes." Suddenly, she was lifted off the ground and swung around.

Maddy and Valentina rushed to her side. "Is this what I think it is? Are you two engaged?"

"Yes." Dominic finally set her on the ground so her friends could hug her.

Tears streamed down her face, so happy everyone was there, especially her new fiancé. "I finally have the happy ever after that I always wanted."

The End

About the Author

Ginger Ring is an award-winning author with a weakness for cheese, dark chocolate, and the Green Bay Packers. She loves reading, watching great movies, and has a quirky sense of humor. Publishing a book has been a lifelong dream of hers and she is excited to share her romantic stories with you. Her heroines are classy, sassy and in search of love and adventure. When Ginger isn't tracking down old gangster haunts or stopping at historical landmarks, you can find her on the backwaters of the Mississippi River fishing with her husband.

Facebook Writer Page:
https://www.facebook.com/romancewritergingerring

Twitter:
https://twitter.com/GingerRings

Webpage & Blog:
http://gingerring.com/

Amazon Author Page:
http://amzn.to/1fslijd

Pinterest:
http://www.pinterest.com/Gingernovel/

Instagram:
https://www.instagram.com/ringginger/

Note From the Author...

I love to write stories that take place in my home state of Wisconsin. The inspiration for the setting of this story is the beautiful tourist town of Lake Geneva. I changed the name to Genoa for the story but forgot that there is a real town called Genoa in Wisconsin. Both are beautiful places to see, so if you ever travel to Wisconsin, make sure to visit both. I hope you enjoyed this Caponelli family story as there is more to come.

Join our Reader Group on Facebook and don't miss out on meeting our authors and entering epic giveaways!

Limitless Reading

Where reading a book
is your first step to becoming
limitless...

LIMITLESS PUBLISHING Reader Group

Join today! *"Where reading a book is your first step to becoming limitless..."*